Touch of a DEMON

AN UNEARTHLY SINS NOVEL

Stefanie Dawn

Touch of a Demon
An Unearthly Sins Novel

Stefanie Dawn

This book is a work of fiction. Any references to real events, real people, and real places are used fictitiously. Other names, characters, places and incidents are products of the Author's imagination and any resemblance to persons, living or dead, actual events, organisations or places is entirely coincidental.

All rights are reserved. This book is intended for the purchaser of this book ONLY. No part of this book may be reproduced or transmitted in any form or by any means, graphic, electronic, or mechanical, including photocopying, recording, taping, or by any information storage retrieval system, without the express written permission of the Author. All songs, song titles and lyrics contained in this book are the property of the respective songwriters and copyright holders.

Disclaimer: The material in this book contains graphic language and sexual content and is intended for mature audiences, ages 18 and older.

DEDICATION

To my readers and everyone who asked for Cade's story. I hope you love him as much as I do.

To be fair, Ashleigh asked for him first, so I have to award her with at least partial custody.

Touch of a DEMON

AN UNEARTHLY SINS NOVEL

PROLOGUE

CADE

Being covered in burning holy oil was an unpleasant way to die, and while I'd known of it being used against demons, seeing him burn like that was the first time I had witnessed a human trying to take an angel's life.

He is an *angel*. What could he possibly have done to make a human want to kill him? And to kill him in such a horrific and painful way? He'd be spending his eternity in Hell reliving the pain he had put that angel through. There was no redemption for the attempted murder of a celestial being.

Zaqiel might forgive him, but I would not.

Without my help, the ashes that were once his body would've blown away in the gentle breeze and consumed him entirely until there was nothing but a memory of where he used to be. To heal Zaqiel, I had to transfer my ability for expedited healing, and it was draining and dangerous to essentially transfer part of my life force to him. I gave as much as I could until I saw the burns shrinking away on his skin, and he was no longer fading away.

All I could bear to share I did. Any more, and I would have died myself. I'd recover but be weakened for a while and extremely vulnerable to injury, which would force me to be careful in a way I wasn't used to—to act more human.

But it was worth it because this angel had cemented a promise with me—a demon—that I insisted one day I'd pay him back for. And today was that day.

With my chin resting on my chest, the woman who had been with Zaqiel was still hanging off his shoulder as he mirrored my pose, and we kneeled in front of each other as though praying together. Zaqiel reached forward and lightly slapped me on the knee, and I could feel the weakness of his movement. But he was alive, and that's all that mattered.

"How did you know?" he mumbled.

"Hey," my lips lifted into a slight smirk, and it was all I could manage with what little energy I had left. It would take everything I had to get up and leave this alleyway now and find a way home, then I could collapse and recoup for days, drawing my energy back until I was whole again. "You know me. Cops around, I'm not far away." My barely-there smirk dropped as I recalled the smell of burning skin singeing the inside of my nostrils. Burning skin, blood, and holy essence. "I smelled the burning holy oil, and I came running, but I didn't know it was you."

I lifted a hand. Whether to take his hand or not I wasn't sure, but moments before making contact, I stopped and simply returned the light slap on the leg that he had given me. "Got here just in time," I muttered as I returned my hand to my lap. The gesture of taking the angel's hand would have seemed too intimate, even for me. It was hard enough sitting here, reliving the act that he had done for me three years ago, saving my life and heart without even knowing he was doing so. To him, it was what angels do, but to me, it was so much more than that. I was in his debt, and demons don't take these things lightly. A life for a life, and as I had now saved him, we were even.

With a great deal of effort, I lifted my head, studying the woman who still clung to Zaqiel. Her hair was dotted with the ash that had been his burning form. His skin continued to heal and solidify as I watched, and I sighed. He was going to be okay.

Raising his eyes to meet mine, he asked, "Are you okay?"

"Yeah," I said, taking a moment to do a mental

sweep of my body. The weakness reverberated through my muscles, and all I wanted to do was lie on the ground and let myself heal. But I'd have time to rest later. "I mean, I will be." The angel was frowning, concern etched on his features. He had been the one who almost burned alive, and *he* was worried about *me.* Typical fucking angel. I smiled. "Don't get all emotional on me. I'll recover."

"Thank you."

This whisper came from the woman, who was staring at me now, her arms still wrapped around the angel, squeezing him next to her. I don't know if she understood what he was or what *I* was for that matter, but the tears that streaked through the grime on her cheeks told me all I needed to know about what she felt for him. My chest ached with a pang, and I was thankful I had been here when he needed me.

Thankful to whom? I wasn't ready to think about that part yet.

"Thank you, Cade. I don't know how I can ever repay you."

Pushing myself to my feet, I chuckled. "You already did, remember?" Brushing a fleck of ash from my jacket, I watched the angel before me. "Now we're even."

CHAPTER
1

CADE

Three Years Earlier...

"You are one gorgeous specimen of a man."

I smirked as Nikki tripped over my feet on the way back to her chair, throwing me a look that indicated it was my fault my feet were at the end of my legs. I steadied her with a hand on her hip, taking the chance to caress her waist, my fingers twitching with the urge to lift her top and feel her skin against mine. While it would have made more sense for her to walk around my chair rather than in front of me, I'm certain she chose to cross over my legs to offer me a good view of her ass before she sat down. She stretched her legs less than gracefully over mine, bending slightly and holding the table, careful not to spill her drink as the curves of her ass were on display for me.

Dropping into her seat, Nikki grinned over her beer before taking a long drink and finishing with an almost comical *ahh*. I still hadn't responded to her and preferred to sit back and listen to her talk. Besides, how does one even respond to a comment like that?

Wanting to listen to a human talk was new to me. I'd had my brother, Nuno, tell me of a similar feeling toward a woman he met in a bar, and I humored him but thought nothing further of it, putting it down to a crush on a woman who had been a great fuck.

Until Nikki.

She'd come waltzing into the bar, dressed in black and fresh from a funeral, looking to drink her sorrows away and perhaps find some company for the night. Nikki had her eyes on me as I spotted her the moment she crossed the threshold. I liked that she was fit and looked as though she'd pose a challenge to any human in a fight, regardless of their gender or build. She was taller than most women I'd met, although she still had to look up at me. I imagined picking her up and throwing her on the bed or taking her against the wall.

Elevated strength had its benefits.

While Nikki was evidently made of something tougher than most humans, the funeral had broken something in her, and it was something she wasn't willing to face yet.

So, she was drinking, talking to a stranger about her job, while throwing in a generous amount of clumsy flirtation. Like she hadn't done it in a while, or perhaps it was part of her charm.

My guess was the former.

And as a cop in a city as messed up as this one, it turns out her job was an interesting topic to discuss.

She tucked a strand of hair, almost perfectly straight, behind her ear as it came loose from her ponytail. Nikki was fighting a losing battle trying to keep her hair up. The tie had slipped too far down, and while it could be tightened, I don't think her fingers could manage the fiddly task with how many drinks she'd been putting away. I wished she'd give up and let her hair fall wild and free to match her mood.

"Nothing to say there, hot stuff?" she prompted me, rousing me from my musings.

Taking a swig of my beer, my smirk was still firmly in place. It was practically my dominant expression by now, amused by humanity and life on the surface as I was. It was nice to feel comfortable here like I never did in Hell. "Nothing much to say to respond to that."

"Don't you want to return the compliment?"

"Did you only compliment me to get one in return?"

"No..." she emphasized the word by slamming

her glass down on the table, "… but it would be gentlemanly to return the compliment."

"You have a very fuckable mouth."

She laughed, drinking again. "Not much of a gentleman, are you?"

"Not that I've been told."

"Fine, I'm not looking for a gentleman."

"What are you looking for?"

She shrugged. "I don't want to think about today. I just want to forget until tomorrow."

"What happens tomorrow?"

"I return to my job, my life, and have to consider the implications of his death."

Should I ask her whose?

She was watching me. "A coworker, if you must know."

Her lip lifted, revealing perfect teeth, her sneer perfectly matching the scorn in her tone. My, wasn't she an open book? She wasn't bothering to hide her hatred for someone, even on the day of their funeral.

But her reaction did beg me to say, "Doesn't sound like you were too fond of the guy."

"I wasn't. He was a crooked cop."

I waited for her to elaborate, but she didn't. "So why are you here drinking your sorrows away over someone you didn't like?"

"I'm not sad about his death, but I'm certain the person who was responsible was also accountable for my father's murder. It just brought up a lot of stuff, okay?"

She was challenging me to push further, but this wasn't a line of questioning I wanted to pursue. Besides the fact she had made it clear she didn't want to talk about it, I was here for a good time, just like her.

I held up my hands. "I'll ask nothing more about it."

She smiled, the frown melting away. "Good, thank you."

My head tilted slightly to the side while I watched her. Humans were fascinating, and it had been several months since I'd decided to take up permanent residence on Earth. There weren't many of us who made the move permanent compared to the total population of demons, but if humans knew how many demons there were on the surface, they'd be disturbed.

No doubt they'd be disturbed by even one.

Although Nuno seems to have found a human who stuck around even after she saw him for what he truly was. But the fear on her face when she witnessed him beginning the change—his eyes yellowing and skin a map of black and bright red— isn't something I took pleasure in.

When I wanted people to be afraid of me, *then* I'd take pleasure in it.

Nikki was talking about work again. I supposed

she didn't have many people to vent to.

Either that or she was drunk.

"Just yesterday, in fact…" she said, slapping her palm on the table, "… some perp made some lude-ass comment about my hair, *ooh did it hurt when you fell from Heaven?*" She made a dry-heaving sound and pointed a finger into her mouth.

"I like your hair," I said.

She rolled her eyes but smiled. "Thank you, but I've only just recently stopped hating it."

"Why would you hate it?"

She dropped her other hand to the table and stared at me. "Do you always ask so many questions?"

My eyebrows shot up, a momentary wave of uncertainty flowed through me—*was I doing something wrong?* Before my swagger returned—demons don't question themselves—I smiled again. "Is that not how you have a conversation?"

"Well… *yeah.*"

She rolled her eyes again, and it was my turn to laugh. "Are you going to answer the question then?"

"Because I am tired of the comments I get about looking like an angel, looking innocent, looking like I could do with *corrupting* and all sorts of other bullshit. It also means people don't take me seriously as an officer… they see my hair and assume I'm a bimbo."

"You're not? Shit, so I've been wasting my time

chatting with you when I could just find some bimbo to get laid?"

Nikki laughed, laying a hand on my arm. "Oh, trust me, you're definitely getting laid tonight."

I arched a brow, taking a drink. "Well, all right then."

Putting my drink down, I leaned forward, scootching my chair across the floor until I was next to Nikki. She watched me, her eyes on mine as I reached behind her, gently undoing the hair tie and sliding it from her hair so her ponytail fell out. Her hair must be naturally straight, because it was left with no kink from the formerly tight ponytail as it fell over her shoulders, so blonde it was almost white. I got it, the comments about her looking innocent and corruptible, but I'm glad she didn't change it.

Because it did make me want to corrupt her, the way her eyes flashed with lust at my touch. I wanted those lips to beg me, to say my name, and to cry out nasty words when she came.

Soon.

"You're beautiful," I crooned.

She chuckled. "I already told you you're getting laid, so you don't have to sweet-talk me."

"So, I wasted my *fuck-me* voice as well?" There was a sharp intake of breath past those gorgeous lips as I ran my thumb over them. Smirking, I dropped my voice again, allowing the seductive nature of my demon to ooze through my tone. We're sexual beings, and sometimes we can't control our effect on humans. They tend to gravitate toward us, drawn by a force they don't understand. But with control, our effect can be switched off as efficiently as it can be ramped up, and although Nikki was already responding to me on a physical level, I let it out a bit more. I wanted her to get wet while sitting here in the bar because I wanted her to be practically squirming and begging by the time I had her naked.

"Mmm…" I hummed, still tracing my thumb across her bottom lip, "… maybe not completely wasted."

She trembled, her light hazel eyes staring into mine. "You're really good at this," Nikki whispered.

"I know."

Nikki chuckled, her voice wavering slightly. She leaned back away from me, and I let my hands drop from her face. She finished her beer, not taking her eyes from mine, her look taking on a hungry quality.

She stood. "Shall we get out of here?"

Finishing my beer, I threw some notes on the table and stood too. Nikki went to move for the door, and I slid an arm around her waist, pulling her in next to me and smirking as she gasped. Nikki could be tough and could look after herself, obviously, having taken on an already-dangerous career in a city filled with criminals.

And demons.

But she still fell apart when I touched her.

Demons had two modes—fucking and fighting.

And damn, Nikki was simply oozing lust. I could smell her arousal and feel it coming off her skin in waves. Pulling her close against my chest, I growled when she trembled, the vibrations sending another shiver up her spine.

"I'm going to need your consent to fuck you until we both come hard," I whispered against her ear, my arm tightening around her waist as her legs weakened slightly. She hummed, her eyes closed, and she put her hand on my cheek again as she searched for my lips with hers.

Brushing my lips against her cheek, a growl rumbled through my throat again. "I'm gonna need you to say it, Nikki. Only once, then later, you can *beg* me."

"Yes," she hissed through her teeth, parting her lips, inviting my tongue into her mouth.

But she'll have to wait.

"Good," I hummed my approval as I moved away, chuckling at her frustrated sigh, before I led her out of the bar.

With one motion, Nikki threw her handbag to one side and her jacket to the other as we walked through the doorway of her small townhouse, squeezed between larger dwellings on either side. Glancing around, I didn't bother trying to contain my amusement. The place was what I could only imagine as organized chaos. Nothing appeared to have a place. Every surface was covered in clothes or papers and any other assortment of items you could think of. Yet I bet if I asked her to locate an item, she'd know exactly where to go. It wasn't dirty, only messy.

This chaotic woman and her chaotic home, I was digging it.

"Welcome!" Nikki cried, pulling her black shirt over her head without undoing all the buttons, revealing a sensible black bra that immediately drew my gaze. She spun on the spot, stumbling over her feet and laughing before she grabbed onto the couch and attempted a seductive lean. It didn't work, looking as much like the drunk tilt it really was, and I chuckled while unzipping my jacket, folding it in half before draping it over the back of the couch.

"You..." she pointed dramatically at me, "... are wearing too many clothes."

I let my gaze wander down her legs, taking in the fitted-into black jeans and low-heel boots. Approaching her, I placed a palm on her chest, and with a gentle push, she fell back onto the couch.

"Oh, any other day you tried that, I would've landed you on your ass."

"I'll take you up on that," I said, unzipping her boots and sliding them off with her socks. Nikki lifted her legs and wiggled her toes in my face.

"Ooh, sweaty toes," she said, falling back against the couch and laughing.

Smirking, I ran my fingers over the bottom of her foot, causing her to squeal and try to pull away, but I held on to her ankle, continuing to touch her sensitive sole until she kicked out at me with her other foot, landing a blow against my jaw.

"Oh my God, Cade, I'm so sorry." She leaned forward and grabbed my face.

I rubbed my jaw, smirking, "Hell of a kick you've got there."

"Did I hurt you?"

"I don't think you could."

She gave me another look of seduction, grinning. "That's something we'll put to the test another day. Right now, you need to get naked and get on the bed."

Standing, I held out my hand, and after Nikki stood, she undid her jeans, shimmying out of them and revealing matching black underwear. She was lean and fit, and after we fucked, I thought I might take her up on her offer for a fight and see what she's really made of.

Not tonight, though. Tonight was all about another form of pleasure.

She wanted to forget today.

I'd make her forget her damn name.

Nikki snatched my hand and led me to the small bedroom. She fell back against the mattress, still laughing while I yanked my T-shirt over my head and tossed it to the side. Once finished undressing, I sat on the edge of the bed, leaning toward Nikki as she sat up. I moved in for a kiss, and playfully she tried to move away from me. With a growl, I grabbed her, tangling my fingers through her hair and yanking her toward me, claiming her mouth with mine.

Her moans were delicious, and I wanted more.

My lip lifted into a snarl when I went to grab her harder, and she pulled away, standing and pushing a hand against my chest.

"Lean against the headboard," she said. She was still chuckling, and I wanted to know what the fuck was so funny, but not as much as I wanted to bury my cock into her tight cunt, so the jokes could wait.

Begrudgingly, I did as she requested. I wasn't one for taking orders, but she seemed determined, so I'd let her play her little game before I took control of her and showed her what true domination looked like.

The little minx climbed on top of me, guiding me to hold onto the headboard, my fingers curling around the cool metal of the bars. She was faster than I'd anticipated, and with a quick motion—I'm surprised she was able to pull off while intoxicated—she'd handcuffed me to the bed.

Smirking, I shook my hands slightly, the metal of the handcuffs rattling against the headboard.

Wait, *metal?* Not plastic, not cheap fake handcuffs.

"Are these real?" I asked her.

Nikki laughed again, nodding. The metal clicked a few more times as she tightened them before twirling the key in front of my eyes and placing it on the bedside table. "Yep, I'm a cop, remember?"

"I don't think you're supposed to use these for sex games."

"Oh, don't be such a prude." She pouted.

She didn't know why this bothered me so much. Fake plastic handcuffs I could break without giving it a second thought—anyone could break those. But metal, legitimate handcuffs, if I broke those as easily as ripping paper, there'd be questions.

And demons weren't good with restraints.

Moving off me, she took her time removing her bra and panties, placing them with a flourish on the mattress next to me in an extra tease before she straddled me again, keeping her hips high so as not to allow my cock the sensation of her wet pussy lips on it. A growl rumbled through my throat, and she licked delicately at my lips, nipping gently before moving away, not letting me kiss her. Her scent was intoxicating. I needed to taste and touch her. I pulled against the handcuffs.

"This isn't a good idea, Nikki," I said, keeping my tone as casual as possible. She was giggling again as she traced her tongue along my neck and down my chest. I tightened my grip against the bars again. "Nikki, you really need to undo these."

"Not until I've had my way with you." She laughed.

Nikki traced her fingers down my chest and over the lines of my muscles, finding the V-shape that led to my crotch, and played with the spot. When she grabbed my already-erect cock in her hands, the metal headboard groaned, and she looked up, smirking at me.

I was going to break the damn bed if she wasn't careful.

Summoning as much restraint as I could, I closed my eyes, moaning as she took me in her mouth, massaging the head with her tongue while she ran her hand up and down the shaft. Her mouth was warm, her tongue working magic over the head of my cock, every brush of it making me jolt as I lost the battle against the urge to thrust into her mouth.

"Fuck..."

She hummed around my cock, the vibrations sending a new wave of sensation through my body. The headboard creaked again, and I released and flexed my fingers, trying to relax, only to grip the metal bars again when she started bobbing her head up and down in my lap with renewed enthusiasm.

"Nikki, please, you don't know what you're doing..."

She released my cock from her mouth with a *pop* and looked at me, frowning. Still stroking my length, she dragged her nails up the skin, rubbing the head with her thumb in small circles. When I groaned again, she said, "Excuse me, I think I know *exactly* what I'm doing."

The muscles in my arms were twitching as I gripped the bars. "No, no, I don't mean that. I mean the handcuffs, you need to let me go."

"You're really bad at relinquishing control, you know that?"

Lowering my head, I stared at her with a darkening expression. "You have no idea."

She moved her face close to mine, making a snapping motion with her teeth as I leaned forward, trying to capture her lips for a kiss. "I think the lesson will be good for you."

Her eyes shifted slightly out of focus as she dived down again, sucking my cock in long, deep pulls with her mouth. The sounds of metal scraping against metal either didn't bother her, or she didn't notice, and the headboard creaked and groaned as I pulled against it.

"Nikki..." I tried one more time to plead reason with her as I moaned, bucking my hips up into her mouth further.

She kept going, and I almost lost control.

Nikki sat up, straddled my legs, and laughed, her chin wet from saliva and pre-cum. With her head tilted back, she rubbed her nipples in front of me, the same shade of pink as the hue that marked her cheeks. She closed her eyes, moaning gently while her head lolled lazily to the side.

I wanted to touch her—*needed* it—because the restraints, coupled with the feel of her heat over my legs, was pushing me to my limit. My demon was screaming at me to take control, to take *her.* Her arousal was in the air, and her scent was driving me crazy, tugging at my willpower to keep my demon under control. I didn't want to hurt her or slip up with my strength and be too rough. I only wanted to bring her pleasure.

But these damn *handcuffs.*

I definitely didn't do well with restraints.

I couldn't wait any longer.

My pupils dilated when I realized what was happening only a split second before it played out. With a roar, I lurched forward, the handcuff chains snapping as I grabbed Nikki, catching her just as she passed out.

CHAPTER 2

CADE

It was probably a good thing she hadn't seen me break the handcuffs. Still, I'd have to find a way to explain to her how they were broken. Maybe I'd take the broken pieces with me, telling her I'd put them somewhere in her home, and she'd just lost them in the mess.

Maybe she'd buy it.

Maybe.

But meanwhile, I was left with an unconscious and naked woman in my arms, tilted back so her breasts were jutting out toward my face. It was a herculean effort to slow my breathing and force my demon under control with the feel of her skin finally under my fingers. She was so soft, and all I could think about was how her pussy would taste.

There are a lot of things that would be the wrong

thing to do in this situation, and licking her cunt while she was unconscious was definitely one of them.

The muscles of my shoulders and back were rippling under the skin, ready to throw her to the bed and fuck her like she'd never been fucked before.

But fucking an unconscious woman did nothing for me. I'd tortured people for that sort of shit back home.

Cursing, I slowly lowered her to the bed. A small smile was on her face as she stretched and rolled, curling into a ball without waking.

"Hope you can forgive me for what I'm about to do next," I mumbled to her passed-out form, running my fingers through my hair.

It wasn't the same, it never was, but I needed to release the pent-up energy.

Taking my cock in my hand, I palmed the length, not bothering to start with slow, steady strokes but simply pumping it hard while the leftover chain of the cuff on my wrist jingled obscenely. Glancing over my shoulder intermittently, I took in the curves of her thighs, her ass, and a peek of her pussy I could see between her legs.

"Fuck," I groaned, increasing speed. Even for me, this felt low—jerking myself off in Nikki's home with her unconscious on the bed behind me. But I wasn't stupid and knew well enough what would happen if I didn't release the built-up tension. I'd risk losing control of my demon, and it was either this, finding someone else to fuck, or shaking her awake and taking her right now. I didn't want anyone else. I only wanted her.

Picturing her lowering herself over me, sliding my cock into her delicious cunt, I groaned loudly, grabbed her panties, and came in them.

Finding my pants, I pulled them on and tucked the sticky panties into the pocket. Using my fingers, I snapped the cuffs off my wrists and headboard and pocketed the broken pieces.

Turning, I faced the unconscious woman on the bed, now looking more like she was asleep and less like she was passed out, her breathing soft and steady, and still with that little smile on those perfect lips. I had the urge to lean over and kiss her, and while my brothers often gave me a hard time for being the quiet, gentle one, that move would be a tad too sentimental, even for me.

Instead, I adjusted her position on the bed, tucking her legs under the sheet and pulling it up over her shoulders. She wiggled and dug herself into the mattress and pillows as though it was a nest, and I chuckled—a really cute move for someone who was a tough cop.

"If you tell anyone I tucked you in, I'll deny it," I whispered to her, certain that the corners of her lips lifted even more before she rolled onto her other side.

Searching around, I turned over a few items before locating a piece of paper and a pen and scrawled out a note to her.

Angel hair,
You passed out, guess you can't handle your booze like you claimed.
Hope you forgot about today as you wished.
Here's my number.
Cade.

It'll do.

Placing the note on the bedside table, I went about finding my clothes and getting dressed, stopping only to have a drink of water direct from the tap and snatch a bag of chips off the counter before leaving.

It was time for me to find the city's local celebrity businessman, Frank.

A demon, but humans didn't need to know that part.

Because if I couldn't get myself under control by fucking all night, then I needed a fight.

Call me a pushover, but something didn't feel right about going out and finding someone else to fuck. Not after Nikki. I doubted I'd find anyone else with her spirit, and nothing less would do now that I'd been so close to having her, only to have that taken away from me.

Besides, demons were territorial, and now that I wanted her and she wanted me, there'd be an almost animal drive within me until I claimed her.

Fuck.

Punching Frank's number into my phone, I held it to my ear, waiting for him to answer as I strolled through the dark streets. Nikki lived in an area bordering the best and worst of this city—it was almost as if you could draw a line and go from one area to another with a single step. The higher end of the city was full of parklands and high-rises, high-end businesses, expensive luxury apartments, and retail outlets. Bordering that was a small middle area of townhouses and restaurants, where the rich came to eat and the poor came to work. Then you came to my domain, the darker side, one area mostly industrial, the other full of apartment buildings cramming as many people into as small a space as possible. Not to mention the throbbing night scene, which kept the crime in the area flushed with dirty money, plenty of people looking for drugs, even more willing to make and sell them.

Nikki had said her coworker was dirty, and I wasn't surprised. Many of the cops here were. I imagined it was difficult to stay pure when you lived in an area so polluted with corruption, it would be easy to be seduced by money and power, regardless of who was offering it.

Despite Frank living in a penthouse apartment at the other end of the city, close to where he worked at one of the largest architecture firms in the state, I headed downtown through the raging nightlife where the area was fueled by crime and illegal decadence and felt more like home.

But I didn't miss Hell.

My inclination to get involved in criminal activity was bordering on nonexistent. Since being on Earth, I'd managed to find steady work as a furniture mover for a boutique custom shop, producing items that seemed much too high-class for the location of the shop in this city. Smithy paid cash, which suited me, and he liked me because I could lift the same as two men.

I could lift more, but I felt I needed to keep what he knew about my strength within reasonable and believable realms. No need to unnecessarily explain to a human what I really was.

On the other hand, Frank had chosen hard work, education, and commitment and had joined an architecture firm started by Mike—another demon, of course—and with them both together, it took off.

Frank answered seconds before I was ready to hang up the call. "Evening, Cade," he said. He sounded out of breath, almost panting.

So I asked, "What did I interrupt? Fucking or fighting?"

"Wouldn't you like to know, you creep?" I could practically hear the wink in his voice.

"I would actually. Nuno mentioned you attend some sort of fight club or some bullshit. I need an outlet, so tell me where to go."

"You're in luck, brother. I'm here now and just finished handing some little fucker's ass to him."

"Didn't anyone ever tell you to pick on someone your own size?"

"Are you challenging me?"

I considered the question. Frank would certainly help work out my desire for a fight better than most demons who were only here for a visit. Earth attracted the younger demons, those seeking a thrill and a fuck, maybe to just mess about with humans on the surface for a change to the tortured souls in Hell.

Frank was older than me and bigger. I was no lightweight, but he was built—an imposing figure that couldn't be hidden by the expensive suits he wore.

Did I want to fight him?

Kind of, yeah.

Siblings tended to fight more than strangers between demons, some sort of built-in need to take each other down, as though there was a battle for nutrients or survival when no such fight existed.

"Yeah," I finally said, ignoring the increase in my heart rate at the thought, adrenaline already kicking in. "I'll fight you."

"You say it as if I asked you on a date."

"Don't be so cocky. I'll give you a run for your money."

"Are we placing bets now too?" Frank laughed.

"Not all of us are rich bitches like you, asshole."

He was still chuckling when he gave me the address—an abandoned warehouse near the edge of the city. I was a handful of blocks away. He added, "Don't be jealous because I live the life even most humans could only dream of."

"Don't wear yourself out on the weaklings." I sneered.

"You should hope I do."

The phone clicked against my ear as Frank hung up.

Increasing the length of my strides, I changed direction slightly and headed toward the warehouse. A fight club seemed a ridiculous thought, but it was better demons got together and tore each other apart rather than lose control and risk hurting or killing a human.

Or several.

There were rules against that kind of thing.

On my way, I concentrated on the feel of my demon, allowing myself to relax the constant control we needed to have, and sensed my muscles ripple with excitement and the promised bloodshed. Frank would be a challenge to take down, and knowing him, he wouldn't give me a chance to warm up, so I needed to walk in there pumped and ready to go, preferably even launching at him before he could me.

The onlookers would place their bets if they wanted. I didn't care.

Shrugging off my jacket as I entered the warehouse, I followed by pulling my T-shirt over my head and discarding it to the side, rolling my shoulders, and punching the air a few times. My breathing was heavy and ragged, and my eyes flashed yellow as I released hints of my demon and approached the group at the other end of the warehouse, passing crumbling pillars and stepping on debris from a forgotten attempt to restore the building.

Frank came from the crowd to meet me halfway, barefoot and bare-chested, only wearing pants that looked to be half of an expensive suit. It took only a beat of a moment for the remaining demons to realize what was going on, as Frank and I, two demons who were older and more powerful than they, stopped a few feet from each other.

My fists were held up level with my chest as Frank rolled his neck, the bones crackling too many times to be human. His eyes never left mine, nor did that smirk of amusement plastered on his smug face. I cared for my brother, but he was an arrogant bastard, always had been, and I wouldn't deny there'd be a certain level of satisfaction at knocking him out.

If I could.

"Welcome, brother—"

Before he finished his sentence, I swung a punch at his jaw, surprised when he managed to lean out of the way. Not quite fast enough, as I felt my knuckles graze the five o'clock shadow on his chin. His eyes flared with yellow and rage at being caught out, and he raised his fists to mirror my stance as I shifted my weight between my feet, wishing I'd removed my shoes too.

Frank launched an attack, and I managed to block most of his blows, copping a few to the ribs and stomach that would've had me buckling over if I had given into the pain. I snuck in a backhanded hit direct to his ear, and his head twisted to the side. But he caught my arm at the elbow and used my momentum against me, hurling me past him and into the dirt and trash that littered the floor.

There was cheering which both Frank and I ignored as I pushed myself to my feet. He was constantly moving from foot to foot, keeping his fists up between us, his knuckles bloodied with his blood or one of the other demons, I didn't know nor care at this point. There was something about having a blood relative so close, something that pumped that need to survive through my veins and forced me to arch my back as my muscles shifted to accommodate a change into my true form I wouldn't allow to happen.

Fight club was done in your human form. I'd been told of the rules, what few there were.

No humans, no killing, and no demon forms.

Although there were more than one pair of yellow eyes in the crowd, and Frank's in front of me, letting some of that power peek through was accepted. Fighting would be pointless if we weren't allowed to let that part out—we weren't here to restrain ourselves.

The rage was rolling off Frank in waves, not only at my proximity and the competitiveness it induced but at my initial attack without bothering to greet him. It had been a long time since I'd seen Frank, and perhaps I had misjudged. Perhaps his time on Earth had humanized him somewhat, and he was expecting a hearty handshake rather than a punch to the jaw.

Studying him now, I looked for existing injuries he had gained from other fights tonight that hadn't fully healed and weak spots I could exploit because demons fought dirty.

There was blood on his neck. Had someone bitten him?

Momentarily, I was torn between elation at finding a weak point and anger at someone else hurting my kin. But I pushed that to the side, shifting my gaze back to his eyes and moving as though I was going to attack in the same manner again. It almost worked, but once again, Frank's sheer size was an advantage. It didn't slow him down at all, and as I moved toward him, he swept to the side, punching me in the back of the neck with strength that had me staggering before kicking my knee out as I was forced to expose my back to him, unable to stop the forward momentum.

My knee hit the floor, and I growled as I stood and spun to face him. The asshole was smiling again. He knew he had the upper hand—years of experience over me in both fighting and controlling himself.

We parried for so long I'm sure the other demons were tired of watching, the crowd visibly thinning as we fought. I was covered in dirt and sweat, bruised with blood dripping from my nose and lips. Frank wasn't looking much better, albeit slightly less out of breath than I was.

My demon was satiated with the violence inflicted, but this was now about preserving what little dignity I had left.

"Face it, Cade, you're a lover, not a fighter." Frank

barely managed to contain his laughter as I spat blood at his feet. "Deep down, you don't actually want to hurt me, and that's your downfall."

"You say it like it's a bad thing."

"It's a human thing, that's for sure, and here, it's a weakness."

Launching at him again, I had let my pride and emotions get the better of me, and Frank hooked an arm around my neck, forcing me to bend over as he pummeled several blows into my stomach. Winded, I dropped to the floor on my hands and knees, coughing. The remaining crowd left, no longer cheering nor giving a shit about the outcome of this fight, and after a moment, Frank sunk to the floor next to me.

"How do you feel?" he asked, placing a hand on my shoulder.

"I fucking hate you," I growled out, shaking his hand off. I was angry and humiliated, feeling less like a demon than I wanted to. Control was one thing, but to have your pride beaten from you by some arrogant son of a bitch was something else.

Frank chuckled. "Good, so it helped then."

Falling back onto my ass, I brushed the dirt from my pants, giving up when it didn't budge. "Yeah," I said, running my hand through my hair. "Yeah, it worked, all under control again."

Frank watched me for a moment, his head tilted slightly to the side. "You doing okay?" The question was genuine, and it was that peek into the inner part of Frank that few demons, and even fewer humans, saw.

"I'm fine."

"You look angry."

I shot him a glare before letting the expression fall from my face. "I don't like losing."

Frank laughed again, standing and holding out a hand, pulling me to my feet. "None of us do, brother, but if you're going to challenge me, you better get used to it."

"Cocky fucker, aren't you?"

He grinned, the smug look a far cry from the award-winning poster-boy smile he uses in magazines and on his clients. I huffed as I smirked, rolling the aches from my shoulders and shaking my hands out. My body was calm, and my wounds would be healed by the time I got back to my apartment.

Whatever they may say about Frank, he always delivered what he promised.

"How's business?" I asked because it was polite to do so.

Frank's smile had returned, now the award-winning one he tossed about to impress clients and women alike. "Booming. Mike set up a strong base, but let's be honest, it needed a more ruthless touch than the by-the-books play Mike seems to insist on, like he can deny his demon or something." He paused to roll his eyes before they flared with pleasure again. "We've moved into a bigger building, and I can assure you it won't be long before *Blackman, Conner, and Associates* are the only name you need to know in architecture."

"Do you get your design ideas from where I think you do?"

Frank smirked again and winked at me. "Looking for a job?"

I shook my head. "Offices aren't the place for me."

He laughed. "Offices aren't the place for demons, period, but we make do. Besides…" he looked down at what was left of his suit pants, "… I'm loving the lifestyle."

"I'll bet."

"You're always welcome to come by."

"So you can show off your empire?" I asked.

"Fuck yes, I want to show you my new throne."

"*New* throne? You never had one in Hell."

Frank chuckled. "No, but here, I can rule a world of my building."

"And Mike's building."

He lifted a shoulder. "He helped some, I guess."

Chuckling, I slapped Frank on the shoulder. "See you next time."

"Next time you want to get your ass kicked, you mean?"

Scowling, I headed toward the door. It was tempting to turn back and take another few chunks out of the arrogant demon, but there was no point in stirring myself up when I had only just regained the control I had lost. But next time, I wouldn't hold back. Not trusting myself to answer, even as I heard his booming laugh echo through the warehouse, I raised a hand and waved with a casual flick of my wrist.

Next time.

I'd have him next time.

CHAPTER
3

NIKKI

With a groan, I rolled over, flopping my arm over the mattress and huffing out as I landed on my back. My eyes squinted while I swatted my hand through the air as though it was going to make the sunlight that streamed through the sheer curtain go away. My alarm continued to beep, insistent that I get out of bed and increasing in volume every second I left it.

I'd learned too many times I couldn't be trusted not to snooze the alarm until I'd left myself with six minutes to get up and shower before having to make the twenty-minute journey to the station. So, I'd moved my alarm clock into the kitchen, turning it up so loud it forced me to physically get out of bed. By then, I was already next to the coffee machine, so I might as well wake up properly with the magic-bean go-fast juice.

Sipping my coffee, I leaned against the counter and surveyed my home. The townhouse was gifted to me by my father—technically my stepfather, my mother having married him when I was fourteen— but Garrett was more of a father than my real dad ever was, so I called him Dad, and we were close. He looked after me as well as he did my stepbrother, never making me feel like I wasn't a true part of the family. Despite my assertion that I was happy to rent, he had been insistent he wanted to provide me with a place to live. Dad wouldn't accept any money, no matter how many times I tried to sneak cash into his wallet, and any transfers I did were sent straight back. It was no secret he was well-off, his business in real estate taking off once he had several commercial buildings under his belt, but I wasn't one for handouts. It was only my love and respect for him that forced me to eventually give up trying to pay him back.

God, I hoped he knew how much I loved him.

He'd put the townhouse in my mother's name and then transferred it to mine at her death due to cancer when I was eighteen, saying he didn't want it in his name for tax reasons. Whatever that meant. I trusted him to know what he was doing. A businesswoman I was not.

While I wasn't the neatest person, even for me, I'd let this place get out of hand. There wasn't a surface that wasn't covered in something. How did one person accumulate so many *things* anyway? What exactly was I doing in what little spare time I had that required such an array of stuff? There were clothes I'd probably never wear because when I wasn't in uniform, I tended to stick to the same five items. There were books I promised myself I'd read and an array of things I'd gotten to distract myself, thinking I could invest my time in crafts and that would be enough to stop me from working on a case I was beginning to fear I might never solve without some fresh leads.

I was no detective—yet—but when the station had signed off my father's death as a suicide, I couldn't let it slide. He wouldn't kill himself, he wasn't the type, and I was certain someone, or several someones, were responsible for his death. There were too many inconsistencies. For one, he didn't leave a note, and he loved my stepbrother and me enough that he wouldn't even consider leaving without saying goodbye.

For three years I'd been looking into his death, and I'd been led around in circles. It had become apparent I knew next to nothing about his business, and what little I did know was leading me nowhere. I knew he owned and rented out commercial buildings across the city, not so much residential that I was aware of, but no one seemed to know anything. Those in the industry who had a flicker of recognition in their eyes at his name refused to talk to me, and I had no detective badge to flash in their face. Most people were smart enough to know I didn't have the rank to be asking the questions I was. I knew a handful of the buildings he had owned, and the ownership had changed hands a number of times since his death before turning to trusts with seemingly no one behind them. There was only so much I could find through public records. Visits to these venues had rendered no additional useful information.

This only further cemented my suspicions of foul play.

Had someone wanted his business? The entire thing seemed to crumble after his death, breaking into smaller factions, names changing, and some parts disappearing entirely. There was no way this went unnoticed, but when investigated, it was all evidently legal transfers with my father's signature in all the right places. But why he'd disband everything and then kill himself within a few months of each other without explanation was a mystery.

Beyond that, how any cop could look at this situation and think nothing was amiss was ridiculous.

Unless they were being paid off.

So, Officer Victor Kim's death, whose funeral I had attended, stony-faced, maybe had gotten greedy. He wasn't the only cop in the precinct who I suspected of being dirty, too many of his reports didn't add up. There was so much going on in this city which made it abundantly obvious it was being run by some underground crime ring. I couldn't get my head around the fact no arrests beyond minor players being picked up had been made or that no real investigation was being done. Drugs were a huge issue here, and yet, there was no task force, nothing.

Yeah, I'd been busy, and investigating fellow cops was something you wanted to keep quiet.

Perhaps Officer Kim had asked for too much money, or he had done something that upset the people who were paying him to look the other way. Blackmail maybe? A crime organization powerful enough to kill a cop and feel they could get away with it would certainly be powerful enough to fake the suicide of a businessman and take his assets, making them disappear in name changes and paperwork.

I needed to keep my mouth shut because I'd been warned more than once that if I didn't stop investigating above my pay grade, I'd be fired, but I liked my job. Despite the corruption that ran through the force, an unfortunate side effect of being in a city like this, I liked to think I could make a difference if only a small one.

Dad was so proud when I joined the force,

although my brother seemed to have a big issue with it and never told me why. I thought my brother and I were close, but I always felt there was a part of him he was keeping hidden. As long as we weren't fighting, though, I was happy because being safe and content in my own home was something important to me, and it was something Dad had offered when he married Mom. Despite them only being married for a few years, he never stopped treating me like family, even after she passed.

If the last thing I could do to honor him was to find who killed him, then so be it.

Strolling back into the bedroom, I stretched my arms above my head as I walked, pausing only to jump in an attempt to touch the light fitting that hung from the high ceiling at the end of the narrow hall. I'd never gotten close, but that didn't stop me from trying every day.

When I went to grab my phone to put some music on, I found Cade's note, snorting with laughter as I read it. *Couldn't handle my booze*, my ass. I'd have to show him how wrong he was one night. He left his number, which I took as a good sign. What I'd gone into with the intention of being only a one-night stand had turned into an enjoyable evening. Before I passed out, that is. God, I was so horny—sex hadn't been high on my priorities until I decided no-strings sex was what I needed to get out of my head for a change, only to get so close before passing out like a weakling. Checking the time, I contemplated bringing myself off before work. My frustration was pent up after last night, having woken without a warm body next to mine nor satisfaction between my legs. I needed release, and being denied it because I had misjudged my drinks was grating against me. I'd be sure to message Cade later and meet up with him, then maybe we could pick up where we left off.

Exactly where we left off.

Unless…

Would it be weird to ask Cade to come with me tomorrow? Going alone was hard, and it never got any easier. I had no idea where my brother was. I hadn't been in contact with him since Dad died, and I couldn't think of anyone else to ask. It had been a while since I'd seen the girls, entirely my fault, I'll admit, and when I did make an effort to see them again, I didn't want a potentially emotional trip to be our first catch-up. Cade seemed quiet and sympathetic beyond his suave and arrogant exterior, and even if he were nothing more than a hand to hold to get me through the day, then it would be better than doing it alone.

Again.

The anniversary of my father's death was difficult, and I had my own way of handling it.

Dressing in my uniform, the only clothes I didn't sling over the back of a chair and let get wrinkled, I slid my weapon into my holster, making sure the safety was still on and the latch was done up. I'd mostly taught myself how to use it. New recruits were taught to undo the latch and flick the safety in two motions, essentially slowing their response time. But old-school cops did it with one motion, and with practice, I'd mastered the move.

Thankfully, I hadn't had to use it yet.

Snatching an apple from the fruit bowl on the kitchen counter, I stuffed it in my mouth and held it between my teeth while I pulled my hair into a ponytail, taking a bite of the tart fruit only after I locked the door. The city was only beginning to wake up, the sounds of traffic shifting in the distance was a gentle hum that played as a backdrop as I made my way down the small alley to the parking garages out back. Hitting the button, the roller door on the single-car garage hummed to life. These townhouses only allowed for one car per property, and those who had more had to find parking blocks away and walk.

Smiling as my little Honda was revealed bit by bit, the roller door jerking and pausing a few times, I tapped the hood before getting into the car. The paint was peeling on the hood and roof, and the once deep blue was looking pale and aged. But she still purred like a kitten when I started her up, and I patted the steering wheel in praise to thank her for not breaking down, even though I hadn't had her serviced in over a year.

"You and me both," I muttered, remembering again the missed opportunity with Cade, that perfect specimen of a man, as the roller door closed behind me, and I pulled into the street.

A girl just can't catch a break.

"Officer," Lieutenant Charles Niles greeted me. He only ever wanted to be called Niles, as neither Charles nor Charlie seemed to suit him, and nodded at me as I passed and dropped a paper bag containing a donut on his desk. Niles smirked at me. He'd been with the force for over twenty years and had been pivotal in my training. I was thrilled when I had been assigned to the same precinct as him, even though I wouldn't tell him—his head didn't need to be any bigger. Although he'd reprimanded me after finding out about my off-the-books investigation, I was lucky not to have made an enemy of him.

Maybe I kept myself in his good books with donuts.

Making my way across the floor, I joined the morning meeting, a few other officers still trickling in as I flung myself onto a chair, waiting for today's jobs to be assigned.

Sergeant Ted Burke strolled in, smelling strongly of cigarette smoke despite him telling his wife he had given it up, and surveyed the room. Not one for greetings, he immediately began to dish out today's duties, teaming people up.

"Sergeant," I spoke up. If looks could kill, I'd be dead where I sat at the way he looked at me. The room went silent because you don't interrupt the sergeant.

Especially Burke.

"Yes, Kline?" he asked, a slow drawl to emphasize his disinterest.

"Is the murder of Officer Kim still being investigated?"

Is it possible for silence to intensify? It certainly felt like it as though the air had been sucked out of the room.

"Officer Kim committed suicide." Burke's voice was tight, and I could see a vein in his temple throbbing. It was only when the one in his neck began to pulsate you knew you were in real trouble.

"But he left no note. He was a type one diabetic, and anyone who knew him would have known that—"

"Kline—"

"How many people know you can kill someone with an overdose of insulin? One full pen of fast-acting insulin would kill hi—"

"Kline, you will shut your mouth *right now*—"

"He had no history of depression, there were no signs, and he made no attempts to get his affairs in order—"

"Or I'll suspend you *indefinitely*—"

"The report said his bank accounts were drained. Why would he—"

"Kline!"

I only shut my mouth then, with the bellow that came from Burke, enough to silence the entire floor. There it was, the vein in his neck looking as though it was ready to burst. His face was red, and his white mustache twitched with irritation. I'd like to stand my ground, but as he stormed across the room and slammed his palms on the table in front of me, I leaned away from his rage. No one asked how I knew about the insulin because nobody wanted to be on the receiving end of Burke's anger.

I knew because my father had died the same way.

Detectives always say they don't believe in coincidence, but no one would listen to me. Either they, too, were being paid off, or they were being threatened to mark it off as a suicide by someone who was. Or they were shit at their jobs. Two deaths, both with their assets and finances liquidated, died of a supposedly self-inflicted deadly insulin dose. It would be easy to do, easier than trying to hang or shoot someone and make it look like they did it themselves.

Coincidence? I don't think so.

Burke's face was close to mine. "The investigation has been conducted by detectives who were in the force before you were a worm in your father's ball sack." I scowled at him, but he continued, "*Shut. Your. Mouth.*"

I sure hope my eyes conveyed what I was thinking.

I'll keep investigating without you, not to mention with a hefty dose of *fuck you.*

Was this whole fucking force corrupt? Or just stupid?

Crossing my arms over my chest, I rolled my eyes as he moved back to the small podium. When he reached the end of the assignments, I was the only one who hadn't been given something.

"Sergeant?" I asked.

He made a big show of turning around as if he didn't notice I was there, a shit-stirring grin plastered on his stupid fat face which I hated more than I did an hour ago.

"The evidence locker needs cleaning and sorting. Get to it, Kline."

Scowling as I pushed myself from my chair, I kept my mouth shut but not my mind.

Fuck you, Burke.

CHAPTER 4

NIKKI

Practically falling into my car at the end of my shift, I'd never been more thankful to have a day off coming up. Not because I'd had to work particularly hard today, shifting boxes and checking labels didn't exactly stimulate my mind or body, I was exhausted because of being bored and left too long with mundane tasks that allowed me too much time to think.

And I suppose some emotional exhaustion I wasn't yet willing to admit to because it had been years, and things were getting on top of me. I didn't want to give up, but the weight of all the unanswered questions sat heavily on my shoulders.

I refused to believe I was looking too much into my father's death. Granted, an insulin overdose was a clever way of going about it, but he simply wouldn't have done it. There were several insulin pens strewn around his desk where I had found him slumped over, but it would only take one fast-acting insulin to put someone into a coma and practically guarantee his death.

Dad would have known this. So why go to the effort of using three or four?

Would he have had the strength to keep injecting after the first one?

And Officer Kim, while I didn't particularly care for the man, had a wife and children, and him dying in exactly the same way, the scene looking to be almost a duplicate of my father's, was too much for me to ignore.

It wasn't too much for the detectives to ignore, though.

Still, I was no closer to anything. They wouldn't allow me access to Kim's financial records to double-check if he was getting payments from somewhere other than work. I had even hoped there'd be some mark left at the crime scene—a calling card of sorts warning others who may get too greedy, if indeed that was the issue.

But these were professionals, and what would be the point in faking suicide if you were going to leave a clue indicating otherwise?

Kim's wife and children had left the city after the funeral, and Mary Anne wouldn't talk to me or tell me where she was going or why. But the fearful look in her eyes when I asked her who her husband worked for, and the way I was quietly shuffled out of the wake, told me all I needed to know.

I needed to keep my head down for a while. Unfortunately, the reality was if I kept rattling cages, I was going to lose my job.

Or worse.

And I couldn't get rid of the additional fact niggling at the back of my neck, like insects on my skin—what about others I hadn't noticed? If not for the connection made with both Officer Kim's and my father's medical history, maybe I, too, would have missed the potential this was something more. But how many other people had been killed by whoever was doing this? It was no secret there was a constant power struggle going on between crime groups, always battling for the largest slice of the proverbial pie. I can understand why my father would have been a target. He owned a lot of real estate—useful real estate—that simply *happened* to be signed over to God knows who right before he *committed suicide.* Nope, I didn't buy it.

Even though my day off tomorrow wasn't for pleasure, hopefully it would be enough for Burke to calm down and not be such a dick when he was assigning jobs.

My thoughts switched to Cade as I ran my hands down my face. It couldn't hurt to ask him about tomorrow. Tucking my phone between my shoulder and ear, I turned the car on to let it warm up while I waited.

He answered with, "Angel," and damn, his voice was smooth, even over the phone.

"Is that your fuck-me voice?" I asked.

Cade chuckled, and my spine tingled. "Maybe."

"Are you free tomorrow?"

"I can be."

"Would you like to come with me to the cemetery?"

"Kinky."

I chuckled despite myself. "No, nothing like that. Look, this may be a weird ask, but tomorrow is the anniversary of my dad's death, and I usually go visit him. I don't particularly want to go alone."

"It's not the weirdest date I've been asked on."

I could hear the smile in his tone, and I returned it. "That's a story I need to hear but another time. Is that a yes?"

"Yeah, that's a yes."

"Text me your address. I'll pick you up."

"See you tomorrow, angel," Cade said, the words breathy.

How did he make everything sound like seduction? From his reaction, I might as well have asked him to partake in an orgy. Sighing and trying to keep my mind off his body, I threw the phone onto the passenger seat and reversed out of the parking space.

It would be nice not to be alone this time.

Dilemma of the day—*do I dress for a date or as if I'm going to a funeral?*

Dad wouldn't care either way, but it was a sign of respect to at least make an effort when I went to see him. It was only once a year, after all. Eventually, I settled on gray wide-leg slacks and a terracotta-color top which, when tucked in, gave me an almost businesswoman look.

I imagined Cade also wouldn't care, but I was wearing simple black clothes when he had met me—only one step short of having a little hat with a black veil for the funeral—so I didn't want to show up to our first date if that's even what this was in jeans and a *My Chemical Romance* T-shirt that was torn, but I loved too much to get rid of.

Shoveling all the stuff from the passenger seat into the back—not rubbish, just more *things* that I seemed to accumulate—I then made my way to Cade's to pick him up. He lived in an apartment building about ten minutes from my place, and when he jumped in, I made no effort to hide I was checking him out—leather jacket and jeans and a black T-shirt.

Damn. Hot.

Now wasn't the time to touch him, but when he leaned over to kiss my cheek, I turned and met his lips with mine. He seemed surprised but didn't pull away, instead turning the chaste kiss dirty and snaking his hand through my hair before pushing his tongue into my mouth. I moaned, whimpering when he broke the kiss. This was neither the time nor the place to be getting raunchy, but I had forgotten how he made my skin tingle simply by being close. Cade stared at me with such intensity when he pulled away, smiling in a way that made my legs turn to jelly.

Then he frowned, reached up again, pulled the hair tie from my hair, and used his fingers to comb my hair around my shoulders.

"What's it with you and ponytails?" he muttered. He looked at my hair with something almost akin to awe, but it could have been something more sinister, judging by how he kissed me.

"What is it with you and my hair?" I failed to keep the scowl from my face and the resulting tone from infecting my voice. I'd had enough of people obsessing over my hair to last me a lifetime. Cade simply chuckled and ran his thumb over my bottom lip before settling back in his seat and pulling on his seat belt. He looked larger than life in my small car, his head almost scraping the fabric on the ceiling and his legs bent even though the seat was as far back as it could go. Yet he still managed to recline and appear somewhat comfortable, and I got the impression there wouldn't be much that would rattle this man.

Once we were on our way, Cade turned in his seat and inspected the back seat of my car. My lips pressed together in a thin line, and while he smirked, most likely noting the mess closely resembled my home, but he said nothing about it.

"No flowers?" he asked.

I lifted a shoulder, keeping my eyes ahead. "Dad wouldn't have wanted flowers. He felt they were a waste of money."

"Romantic."

I threw him a look, only to relax when I saw the smirk still firmly planted on his face. He was messing with me again. "I brought a picnic, though."

"Seriously?"

"Yep, hope you like quiche."

"Nothing makes me feel more like a man than eating quiche."

"I have dainty little decorative forks too."

"Good, I'll remember to keep my pinky up."

I laughed, and my stance relaxed further. I shifted in my seat, not even sure at which point in the conversation I had begun tensing up. I still didn't know Cade well, and perhaps I was on edge, wondering if he would make fun of me for the way

I grieved. Hell, I could handle teasing—I wasn't a child—but this was a sore spot, and I tended to be on edge the moment the topic came up, preparing myself for a verbal joust I felt was inevitable.

Rolling my shoulders, I threw another smile at Cade, glad that I had asked him to come along and even more so that he had accepted. Nothing about his face or responses beyond the casual teasing indicated he thought it was weird I had packed a lunch for us. This wasn't just a five-minute trip for me to mutter a few words of prayer and leave. I booked this day off every year, and I'd simply sit at Dad's grave for hours. Sometimes talking, other times simply lying in the sun and reading if I remembered to bring a book. It seemed unusual compared to what I knew of others who had their annual rituals to mourn those passing, and I couldn't help feeling my girlfriends might judge me for my odd behavior.

I hadn't ever asked them. Mom would say I wasn't even giving them a chance to really know me. I kept my friendships fairly superficial. This wasn't news to me.

I liked to have fun when I caught up with the girls and not talk about all the shit going on. Sue me.

This time, since I had company, I thought I'd bring a picnic. I didn't see what was weird about it, but I can imagine some people would think it odd. While I was close to my mother as well, she had wanted her ashes returned to Ireland to be spread over the Cliff of Moher, where she used to spend time with her parents, so an annual trip wasn't an option. One day I'd go visit that spot, though.

It was much too early to ask Cade if he wanted to come to Ireland with me. Just because it had been a while since I had someone I'd even consider asking, it didn't mean I needed to come on too strong.

"Well, you're going to love this. I also brought sparkling wine and orange juice so we can make mimosas."

Both his eyebrows shot up at this. "Are we visiting a graveyard or an outdoor concert? What's with all the hurrah?"

I lifted a shoulder. "I make a day of it, and it's nice to spend some time in the quiet."

"Wouldn't you rather be alone?"

His question didn't sound as though it were driven by any malice but more genuine curiosity. In fact, it was hard to picture Cade being malicious about anything. He was so composed and carefree as though he was here to watch the world pass him by without a single care in the world. Hopefully, the attitude was catchy. I wouldn't mind some of it in my life.

I thought of Officer Kim and the questions it raised, and I thought of Burke and other cops who were dismissive of my theories. No one seemed to care about my dad, not even my stepbrother, wherever the fuck he was. The more time that passed after Dad's death, the more my desire to solve his murder intensified. However, I was hit with dead end after dead end, and I'd already pushed away what few friends I had with my ramblings and unwillingness to let it go for even one night so we could go out. When one of them contacted me recently to arrange a catch-up, I got the feeling we were both steadfastly avoiding the topic of my work or my family. Maybe it was just my imagination.

But I didn't want to be alone anymore.

"Not this time," I muttered.

Cade nodded, and not wanting to let the conversation lull, I worked my confidence up to ask what could be an uncomfortable question, given my broken memories from the other night.

"Cade?" I started.

He hummed, turning his head from the window where the city life was thinning as we moved into the suburbs. The graveyard was on the outskirts of the city, a quiet area bordered by country roads that led to the small towns surrounding our bustling metropolis.

I cleared my throat. "Did you take my handcuffs with you the other night?"

He took a moment to answer, and when I tossed a glance his way, he was smiling, his chin resting on his fist and hair shifting around his face slightly from the air conditioner, and I won't deny I took a moment to check him out. The urge to pull the car over and trace my fingers along his jawline and down his neck was strong, stronger than I'd admit out loud. While Cade gave off almost gentle-giant vibes, he oozed masculinity and drew me to him, and I wondered what animal lingered underneath that calm façade and if he'd come out to play in the bedroom.

"I put them in your living room," he said.

Cringing at the memory, I said, "I'm sorry about the other night. If you hadn't been able to get out of the handcuffs after I passed out, there'd have been trouble for the both of us."

He shook his head, smiling. "It's fine. There was no issue, and we're all good. No sense in worrying about something that didn't happen."

Yeah, there are plenty of things to worry about that *did* happen.

"I enjoyed talking to you at the bar," I offered, trying to clear some of the awkwardness I felt, and judging by Cade's face, it was completely one-sided. He didn't seem bothered in the slightest I had left him handcuffed to my bed while I passed out.

What a fucking disaster of a date.

And for our second date, I was taking him to a graveyard. I pulled a face.

"What you can remember of the conversation anyway," he smirked.

I made a *pfft* sound with my lips because I knew he was right and didn't want to admit it.

CHAPTER
5

CADE

Nikki and I chatted as she drove, and I made a mental note to remind myself to offer to drive back. Just because I was stronger than humans and healed faster doesn't mean I wanted to be in a car accident. Every time I tried to let the conversation lull so she could concentrate, she'd look at me and smile, and it would be impossible not to return the expression. But she drove like she was playing a cop in a movie and chasing some perp, swerving around corners way too fast, the sound of the tires on the road breaking the otherwise calm silence of the suburbs. She got almost a manic look in her eye when she took off from the lights, and I swear, in her head, she *was* in one of the cop movies.

Fuck, she was hot.

The whole wanting to corrupt her because she

looked innocent thing, I totally got it. She kept tucking her hair behind her ear as it fell in front of her face because I had taken out her ponytail. What I really wanted to do was bend her over and bunch her hair up in my fist, exposing her neck to me while I fucked her.

Something told me she wouldn't be up for fucking in the graveyard, so I'd have to be patient on that front. But I figured she'd be worth the wait. She was driven and stubborn but with an element of silliness that made me chuckle.

I wondered if she'd orgasm harder if I tickled her while stimulating her, given how she reacted when I got hold of her foot. I wanted to hear that laugh broken with moans and to feel her nails dig into my arms and shoulders as she completely lost control. Since she was the sort to try to restrain *me*, I'd need to set the balance of power right.

Demons don't play submissive well.

My mind wasn't entirely one-tracked. I was actually paying attention to the conversation.

There was a small parking lot next to a stone church that appeared empty, no sound or light emanating from inside and an eerie hollowness to the open windows. While I'd hardly burst into flames if I stepped foot in a church, I didn't particularly want to venture inside either. Something about that felt fundamentally wrong like I'd be giving God a big middle finger *ha-ha, I'm on*

Earth, sucker.

Wasn't my style.

Nikki wasn't here to pray, though, and like the fucking gentlemen I am, I took the picnic basket and carried it as she led me across the field of graves. The sun was out, and I watched her ass as she moved in front of me more than I paid attention to the scenery.

The graveyard shifted from a field littered with plaques, tombstones, and small memorials to an older part of the cemetery I assumed, where the grass wasn't as green, and the stones were thick with moss. Perhaps an old family plot of theirs.

Laying a blanket out on an empty space, Nikki sat and leaned against the back of a traditional-style arched gravestone, marbled and clean, although she rubbed a few flecks of mud off it before settling in. Indicating the stone she leaned against with my chin, I asked, "Is that him?"

She nodded, patting the stone. "Yep. I don't like to sit on top of the grave itself. It's creepy."

"But if we sit here, I'll be sitting on top of..." I glanced behind me, "...*Melissa Wright, mother, wife, daughter, died May 29, 1980.*"

"I'm sure she won't mind having your firm ass planted on her legs."

Chuckling, I removed my jacket and sat, watching as Nikki unpacked what appeared to be a small feast from the basket. "How many people are you feeding?"

"Just you and me. Zombies only eat brains... everyone knows that." She smirked at me. "But I figured you might be one of those guys who eats a deceptive amount comparative to his build."

Lifting my arms, I flexed. "Gotta keep up the kilojoules."

While she laughed, her gaze trailed along my arms and over my chest before returning to my eyes. I didn't need to say anything. The way she hastily looked away told me she knew I'd seen her wandering gaze. Hell, I welcomed it. The more she thought about my body, the better, then maybe when it came time to finally fuck her, she'd be trying to shred my clothes off as much as I'd be hers. After unpacking a few more items, her eyes flashed to my arms again, and I flexed, bringing out another smirk from her.

When she had everything laid out and was serving up a plate for me, I rolled to the side, kicking my legs out, and rested on an elbow, watching her. "You okay?" I asked.

Her hands paused in her work, her lips pressing together in a thin line. "Why do you ask?"

"We've been joking around a lot, but you asked for company because this can't be easy for you. I'm just checking."

The sun sent a cascade of colors across her hazel eyes I hadn't noticed in the bar's dim lighting. Her pale skin meant everything else stood out, including what freckles I could see and the almost permanent slight red flush on her cheeks.

Angel indeed.

She cleared her throat. "It's nice to have company." Lifting her eyes to mine, she handed me the loaded plate. "I've spent a lot of time brooding lately... it's nice to relax." Patting the gravestone behind her again, she added, "I think Dad would want me to be happy."

"Of course, he would."

She pressed her lips together again, nodding only once, and I wanted to know what she was thinking. She'd mentioned in the bar her father had been killed, so maybe she felt she had somehow failed him by not finding whoever was responsible.

But although the bright sun not hindered by clouds exposing a blue sky was misleading, there was no forgetting this was a dark city full of dark people, and who knows who her father could have crossed paths with? If he had something of value, there was no shortage of people who would take an innocent man's life if they wanted what he had.

And if that was the case, she's lucky she was left alive.

The food was good, and I wanted to ask if she'd made it herself, but I was too busy shoveling it into my mouth. Flavors exploded on my tongue in a way they didn't in Hell. Every sense was enhanced on

Earth. The sun warmed my skin but didn't burn, and the cotton of the picnic blanket was delicate. If I closed my eyes, I could focus my senses on one thing or all of them and let everything flood my mind until I was overwhelmed with how pure everything felt.

This is why I was staying on Earth.

I was a demon out of place in Hell, and while there were aspects to my being that, I'd never rid myself of the desire and craving to fuck and for violence and blood—I didn't really want to lose them. I embraced those and had no issues in fighting at the slightest encouragement. There weren't many in the city who didn't deserve a few good punches to the gut and face anyway, and I was more than happy to provide. But the people, the *women*, were something else. Demon females were great, but human women were soft and responded to every touch like it was their first.

It was fun to ruin them for all other lovers.

But beyond the sex and the sensations that Earth offered, there was freedom.

Freedom from the rules of Hell, and short of going around killing people, I could do pretty much as I pleased here. The downside which put most demons off was that life on Earth required a certain level of responsibility—finding a job and some financial stability—unless you wanted to grow weak and starve or steal everything, which had risks of its own. I didn't know of many demons who had taken it to the nth degree as Frank and Mike had, building a business and empire and living it up with the best life Earth had to offer. That shit took some serious commitment, and there were few demons willing to put in the time.

I can't imagine having a job where I needed to wear a suit.

While Frank gave me a hard time when I needed to fight, he knew me better than most and understood I simply didn't fit in in Hell. I didn't fit in on Earth either, but at least I could relax a bit more here.

In Hell, I was a freak, too quiet and timid to get into the hard-core torture.

And when I experienced those painful memories with the humans, the ones I could draw out by tasting their blood on my tongue, the ones we used to psychologically torture, those memories hurt me too. The humans in Hell were nasty people who had done unthinkable things, and while they deserved every ounce of torture they got, I didn't take pleasure in it like most did.

What did that make me? Not much of a demon.

But I wasn't human either.

Earth offered freedom, even if it was governed by other rules. It was freedom to be whoever I wanted to be, and that was something not awarded to me below the surface.

If my desire to be myself made me less of a demon, I'd like to say I could deal with that, but to a point, it bothered me. I'd spent most of my life feeling inferior. At least on Earth, I was stronger, taller, and faster than most.

I was also more violent with tendencies that weren't human.

It wasn't an easy balance to maintain.

When I asked Nikki if she was okay, it was because despite her smile and laugh, I could sense the misery from her, and beyond the misery was guilt. These things were in my nature to pick up on, so I could pry them apart and make it worse for the victim I was torturing.

I didn't want that, not for Nikki.

My attention was dragged back to reality by Nikki's laugh, and I stopped midchew to raise my eyes at her. "What?"

"You eat like it's your last meal."

I shrugged, swallowing. "It's good food."

Her smile was radiant. "Well, thank you. I'll take that as a compliment."

"Exactly as it was intended."

I made a point to slow down as I finished my meal, one step short of licking the plate before placing it on the blanket and rolling onto my back, squinting at the sky.

"Thank you, Nikki," I said.

"For the food?"

Rolling my head to watch her as she packed the basket away, I said, "For inviting me."

"I'm glad I did. I can't imagine many who would be thrilled at the prospect." She relaxed against the gravestone, sighing, "You seem downright relaxed here."

"I'm relaxed everywhere." *Lies.* I was never relaxed in Hell. "Tell me about your dad," I said.

Nikki tilted her head so her cheek rested against the stone. It was strange the importance humans put on inanimate objects to remind them of those they loved.

"He treated me differently."

"From your brother?"

"From everyone." She sighed. "He welcomed me into his home when he'd married my mother, and I never felt I wasn't a part of the family. He absolutely doted on me, but it was never about the things he could buy me, although I still love that car." She glanced in the direction of the parking lot as if she could see the little Honda. I couldn't, so there was no way she could. "But it was like he wanted to teach us to be the best people we could be. We'd play games in the evening instead of watching TV, games that involved problem-solving." She tapped her forehead, and I smiled. "And he always wanted to know how school was and get involved in whatever hobbies I had at the time." Nikki laughed. "Honestly, I've been through so many hobbies I don't even know what I enjoy doing in my spare time anymore."

"Sounds like a great father."

"The best," she replied, and for the first time that day, I heard the emotion break in her voice. Through her entire speech she was biting at her bottom lip, and when a spot of blood appeared, I sat up, handing her a napkin from the basket. She dabbed her eyes with it and frowned when I took it from her and held it against the blood on her lip.

What I really wanted to do was lick it off. Blood was a drug, and the blood of someone so pure and fucking beautiful would be ecstasy as it slid down my throat. If I sucked on her bottom lip, I could draw the elixir into me, and thoughts of fucking her while I tasted her blood invaded my mind.

"Sorry," she muttered as I tried to keep the napkin still while she talked. "Bad habit."

"We all have them."

She watched me, and after a moment when her lip had stopped bleeding, she asked, "What are yours?"

"My what?"

"Bad habits."

Smirking, I held a glass to her and lifted the bottle of wine. She nodded, then took over when I hadn't bothered with the orange juice. It seems she was determined on mimosas. "I'm just too darn handsome," I said.

Nikki laughed, and desire prickled in me. My fingers clenched on the picnic blanket as she got the drinks ready. We'd come so close to being together the other night, and I wouldn't be able to deny myself release for much longer without risking exposing my demon. Control was something that took time—lots of time—and while I had pretty good control since residing on Earth these past few months, it wasn't enough to be able to keep control when I came so close to claiming a woman, only to have that taken away from me. Especially when every little movement she made only increased my need for her—the way her fingers delicately traced over the line of the champagne glass stem and how her lips pursed slightly as she took a sip, her subtle pink tongue darting out to catch the droplets of liquid on her lips.

Lips that had been around the head of my cock.

Demons were territorial. Once we had our sights set on someone, if that interest was reciprocated, we didn't want to seek someone else until we had them.

Shifting my legs, I covered my arousal.

She scoffed. "Really, tell me."

"You want me to sully our first date by telling you my bad habits?"

"Yes, because you're just *too darn perfect.*" She dropped her tone, and if that was meant to be an impression of my voice, it was terrible.

"Fine," I said, accepting my drink and getting comfortable again. "I fight."

"How do you mean?"

Lifting a shoulder, I took a gulp of my drink. Wait! *This was a mimosa?* Why had I been avoiding these? Probably because they sounded too girly. Damn. "As in, I fight. I like to fight. I get together with a group of guys, and we beat each other up. It gets messy." I flexed my hands, and my knuckles cracked, remembering the feel of them collecting someone in the gut.

Her jaw tensed. "Is that legal?"

"You tell me."

She pursed her lips and opted not to answer. "Anything else?"

"Damn, that's not enough? Okay, apparently I eat as though I'm starving. My table manners suck."

Nikki laughed again, and I relaxed as she did, her shoulders dropping as she brought the glass to her lips for another sip.

We talked and sometimes simply sat in silence, and the hours went by faster than I had realized. When I looked up again, the sun was getting ready to drop below the treeline, casting long shadows across the graveyard, making the trees in the distance appear to reach toward us, ready to drag us into their depths.

"We should get going," Nikki said.

Reluctantly, I agreed. This was about her anyway

and wanting to spend this time with her dad, despite him being six feet under, although I felt I had taken up all of her attention. But maybe that's what she wanted. After we had packed up, Nikki stood and moved around the front of the grave, trailing her fingers along the stone as she stepped around the border of the grave.

I followed, keen to stay close to her and curious about what she'd get engraved on the gravestone of someone who meant the world to her.

But once I saw it, the air was punched from my lungs. I coughed, trying to regain myself. My stomach might as well have been filling with lead, and the picnic basket suddenly seemed heavier than it did a moment ago. Or was it my arms that were heavier?

No. It was guilt.

Guilt was heavy on my shoulders, in my gut, and running through my veins.

Guilt.

Because I knew that man, although by a different name.

I knew the face in that little oval photo embedded in the stone.

The man she loved so much, the man whose justice she was fighting for. I knew him.

Ah, fuck.

I had tortured Nikki's father in Hell.

CHAPTER
6

CADE

All thoughts of fucking Nikki had been unceremoniously shoved from my mind, and it took a great deal of willpower to keep my breathing steady, even as my heart thumped in my chest so loud I was surprised she couldn't hear it. She was still caressing the gravestone and had kneeled in front of it, whispering a few words to the man who was her father. A man who could no longer hear her.

He was more than only six feet under her shoes. He was under the surface, in another world, filled with pain, unfulfilled desires, and torture. It was a world full of all the things humans dread to think about and simply hope their images of Hell aren't true.

They are, for some.

My grip tightened on the basket, the cane squeaking under my fingers.

The man she had told me about, who loved her, looked after her, and treated her like a princess was *not* the man I had known.

Garrett Porter.

That wasn't his real name, only one of his aliases, and apparently the one he had been killed and buried with. He was better known under the name he made famous through cruelty and violence.

Mitch Murphy.

He was no property mogul, no regular real estate broker, or whatever the hell he had told her he did for a living. It was all a lie, a cover. I knew this because I knew the man—intimately—all his history, secrets, and deepest fears. Not once in sharing his memories through the transfer of blood had Nikki's face come up, not *once*, which meant all the memories he had of her were good ones. Things I didn't need to know because they wouldn't assist in his torture. I only needed the things that hid in the darkest recesses of his mind, the parts that would torture him when he was forced to be reminded of them.

It was a relief that Nikki wasn't one of these things.

There's no way Nikki, the Nikki who loved being a cop, who wanted to fight and help the good guy, who hated corruption, could know who her dear old dad really was when he lived.

I swallowed, my throat dry. "You have different surnames."

She nodded, her back still to me. "When Mom married Dad, I didn't take on his name. I have my Mom's maiden name which she changed when I was little after she divorced my birth father."

"Oh." It was all I could manage to get out, and my throat felt like it was closing up. The bile in my stomach was making itself known, and I wished I hadn't eaten such a large meal.

There are a handful of crime syndicates in this city, but the largest by area and employees had been Murphy's. He had many rivals and even more enemies. *Of course,* he had been murdered. Men like him rarely lived to die of old age. Hell, he probably even made enemies within his own ranks. He was a cruel man with cruel intentions.

What do men with power crave?

More power.

He harbored little to no guilt for his actions, and so his torture in Hell was mostly based on physical pain rather than psychological. But demons can still learn a lot from humans by tasting their blood— we'll get their memories, and it builds an image of a person that can only be trumped by being inside their mind.

But one thing was clear.

Nikki didn't know who he was.

Clenching and unclenching my hands, I stared hard at the gravestone, knowing that under the stone and dirt were the balls of the man who I had made scream with long, drawn-out, painful deaths over and over again.

And what of the daughter he doted on?

What did Nikki do to spark such a soft side within him?

Because I know for a fact, he didn't treat her stepbrother the same way, not before Nikki came into the family and certainly not after. It didn't surprise me that he didn't bother to keep in contact with her. She was an intruder in the family who he'd have forced himself to be civil around for the sake of a powerful and violent man he called Dad. She got the attention, the love, and the upbringing he should have had all along.

And I thanked God her stepbrother had simply opted to not contact her rather than taking out his resentment on her.

Fuck. Was her stepbrother part of the family business? Was he carrying it on?

What was it about Nikki that made Mitch soften so? Did she remind him of someone? Was it purely her looks all over again? Her soft, beautiful, angel-like features and hair. Surely not. Did she look like her mother? I had never asked. Maybe he truly loved the woman, and perhaps she had broken through into some side of him that hadn't seen the light in many years. The only way to know would be to ask him, and I had vowed never to return to Hell, so that was out of the question.

Why he treated her with such reverence was irrelevant. But now Nikki sought the person who had killed him, and now I knew who her father was, I had no doubt she was correct, his death was no suicide. Did she know that she could potentially be going after some dangerous people trying to find who was responsible?

Sighing, Nikki turned to face me, the little red flush in her cheeks a bit brighter and her eyes shining with tears she was holding back. But she was smiling, and I knew that smile was for me. It pleased me to know that my company had made this day easier for her, and I shoved the horrifying realization of her father's identity aside because while I was with her, I wouldn't let it taint our time.

Dammit.

As Nikki started walking, I turned away from the gravestone, unsuccessfully trying to push Mitch's face from my mind as I strolled next to Nikki. She was in no rush, ambling lightly throughout the graveyard as we moved from the older cemetery back to the open field. My arm brushed hers as we walked, and she lifted a hand to trail her fingers down the inside of my forearm. I shivered under her touch because now, aside from controlling my demon, I was also trying to control my thoughts.

An impossible task.

When she took my hand, I had to resist the urge to yank my fingers from hers when she intertwined them. The gesture was too innocent, too pure, and made guilt and bile swell up in my throat. It wasn't that I didn't want to touch her, I still did, more than ever. Now we were treading in dangerous territory, and she was awakening elements of my nature that simply shouldn't be directed toward a human.

Because beyond the guilt, something else flared inside me.

Possessiveness.

I had seen the man she so loved up close and personal in a way that would make her skin crawl, and battling inside me was a desire to tell her the truth and a stronger desire to keep her safe. To keep her not only from the truth about her family but from the world that created men like her father. I knew she already had seen too much darkness in her job—impossible to avoid. But my desire was to simply throw her over my shoulder, take her to my home, keep her to be mine and mine alone, and spend our days lost in each other's embrace as I claimed her, driving into her over and over again.

My angel.

Possessiveness is a dangerous thing for a demon.

Keep her safe from the world. Take her away with you.

We're territorial beings, persistently pursuing a

female until we are able to claim them. Not against their will, it was never about taking them purely in a physical sense. But it was the chase, knowing that from that first spark between you that she wanted you too, and then having her body under your hands and giving her pleasure she's never dreamed of.

I was territorial over Nikki. I couldn't help it. She had given herself to me willingly and then the chance was snatched out from underneath me. The time we spent together today opened another side of her to me, and vice versa, and I was starting to feel things that could almost be a crush.

Feelings.

If demons experienced such things.

But protective, possessive, and territorial—I was all of the above.

The demon within me raged at her touch, at the simple feel of her fingers in mine, and I had to control myself not to crush her hand with unbridled power. I wanted to take her right here on the grass, not caring if anyone saw or that the setting was far from what a human would consider appropriate.

I needed her now on a level I didn't before.

But I had a past with her father that she knew not of and could never know.

So while I internally battled with guilt and self-loathing, sparks still crawled across my skin at the contact between us. When I squeezed her hand, she

returned the gesture, and my chest tightened.
I'm not sure I could stay away from her.

CHAPTER
7

NIKKI

Once again, I was assigned to clear and reorganize the evidence locker. Burke obviously still had a stick up his ass from my outburst the other day. While I had managed to keep my mouth shut this morning, although I had to grind my teeth through the meeting and satiate myself with images of launching myself across the table at him, the man wasn't going to let it go that easily. If I wanted to keep a decent standing at the station, I'd need to keep my mouth shut for longer than a single day. Long enough, in fact, that he'd believe I had let the issue go, and I doubted that would be done within a few days or even weeks. But three years had been a long time to suck it up, and it started to grate on me. I needed better resources, and I couldn't do it alone.

So, I was stuck working in the station, refused

even traffic duty, and trapped inside a dusty room while the sunlight streamed through the high window, teasing me with its warmth. It wasn't a punishment as such, the work needed to be done and was important, but it was no secret that Burke assigned certain tasks to those he didn't like, and his message was clear.

"Kline."

I looked up at the voice and managed to keep the scowl from my lips. "Torres," I replied, nodding at her.

Karolina Torres often worked with Officer Kim, and she'd made no secret of her distaste of my performance the other day. After the morning meeting she'd demanded I look for files she knew damn well weren't stored in our precinct and then insisted I had somehow misplaced them. She was one of the two officers who had not so subtly escorted me from Kim's wake after I asked his wife a few questions. "Did you enjoy your day off to mourn your father's suicide?" she asked.

The comment was unnecessary and obvious bait. Unfortunately, it turns out I didn't have the willpower to let the remark slide without saying something back. "Murder," I muttered.

She smirked, knowing exactly what she was doing. "It was signed off as a suicide."

I should have been a stronger person, strong enough to resist some petty teasing. It wasn't the first time, and it certainly wouldn't be the last. Of course, it happened when you made an outcast of yourself and insisted an investigation was done incorrectly, the implication heavy of foul play within the force floating around every conversation but never quite verbalized. But I was raw from yesterday, from the reminder another year had passed, and I could find no reason why a clearly experienced killer would target my father. Sure, he had property, but so did a lot of people. Why him? Without a clear motive and help from the resources I should have access to as a cop, I was running in circles.

I was letting him down, and time was draining from my life around me. Finally, I had actually reached out and grabbed on to someone—Cade— and I didn't plan on letting him go as long as those sparks flared between us, his easy smile making my legs weak. But I had already damaged several friendships because I wouldn't let the case go, and I couldn't help the guilt that bubbled in my stomach, feeling as though I was being selfish by wanting a life.

But I also demanded justice for my father.

So, foolishly, I took the bait. "I don't care what it was signed off as, I knew my father. What do you want, Torres?"

"Just helping one of the detectives with a *current* case, and it might be related to one from a year ago.

I need the evidence box for 12-1-00193-3.”

Casting a glance around, I gritted my teeth, trying to convince myself it was a coincidence she was asking for that box at this exact moment when it was clear I was midway through organizing that shelf, and the boxes were strewn across the floor. It was organized chaos, but I had them in a certain order so I knew which order to put them back on the shelf. Moving one now would throw me.

I don't believe in coincidences.

Bitch.

Plastering on a smile I hoped looked as fake as it felt, I said, “Sure thing.” I stepped awkwardly over the boxes to find the one she needed. Placing it on the table, I moved to sign it out to her, and after she scribbled her name on the page, she muttered something.

“What was that?” I asked, sickly sweet and dripping with malice.

Her smile told me what I needed to know before she spoke. She was going to test me again.

Don't take the bait.

“I said…” Karolina started, her shit-stirring grin looming. What the fuck did she know that I didn't? Why was she bothering to torture me with this? I found it difficult to believe this was all because of her loyalty to Kim. To me, Torres was just as corrupt as he was. She licked her lips before continuing, savoring the moment of torturing me.

"Maybe your father shouldn't have assumed his empire would never fall."

She knew something.

I wasn't strong enough to be the bigger person, and I snapped. Grabbing her shirt collar, I yanked her forward until we were face to face. "What the fuck did you say?"

Her smirk waivered at my aggression, realizing a moment too late at our physical difference—while I was younger, I was taller and fitter. Once again, I was underestimated, and this time it worked in my favor. A hint of fear sparked in her eyes as she replied, her voice small and lacking the glee from a moment before. "You heard me."

Tugging her down, I held her in a headlock under my arm, and when she tried to break free, I twisted her arm painfully until she cried out. "Tell me what you know," I said, gritting my teeth as she dug her nails into my arm, trying to squirm out of my hold.

"Kline!"

Fuck.

Releasing Karolina, angry tears stung her eyes as she stumbled away, and I glared at her even as I faced Burke, lowering my eyes to the floor. I was in deep shit. "Sir."

"Don't you *sir* me, Kline! Someone tell me what the *hell* is going on in here?"

"She attacked me, sir." Karolina stood with her back straight, angry red marks appearing on her neck as she rubbed it.

"She said—" I started.

But it didn't matter. I'd already made an enemy of the sergeant on more than one occasion. Besides, her baiting me really wasn't a reason to attack, I knew that. I had no defense, and I was about to pay for my lack of willpower.

"I don't give a goddamn what she *said*, Kline," Burke bellowed, my name sounding like an insult from his lips. "We don't tolerate violence in this precinct." Karolina's face was barely containing her smug expression, and I scowled as Burke continued, "Apparently, you've got too much going on in your personal life to conduct yourself in a professional manner here. Take some time. Effective immediately, you're suspended—"

"Sir!"

"For four weeks. One more word from you, Kline, and I'll double it. Now go downstairs and sign over your gun and badge."

My mouth hung open, and I stared at him.

"Just one word, Kline..." Burke muttered, eyeing me, daring me. "Give me a reason."

Closing my mouth, I said nothing, hoping I could glare the man to death.

After a beat, he hollered, "Dismissed!" and Karolina marched out of the locker room with the evidence box, leaving me to skulk past Burke before he followed, making sure I went straight to administration to sort out my suspension.

They asked where my handcuffs were, and I told them the truth—they were at home, and I hadn't found them due to recent renovations.

Okay, only partly true.

Burke's face turned a new shade of crimson at my confession. Losing police property was no laughing matter, and I ground my teeth, hoping the guilt wasn't written across my face.

Because right up there with losing police property on the list of things you should absolutely not do was using it for kinky sex games.

What was I thinking?

After stomping my way through the parking garage in what I know was a childish show of emotion, but unable to stop it, I drove home in a rage, pulled into my garage, and tilted the seat back in my car. Staring at the car ceiling as the roller door finished closing, I was encased in almost complete darkness. I picked at a loose thread on peeling fabric as I dialed my phone, feeling the weight of the situation wash over me, my anger dissipating into despair.

"Nikki." His voice was as smooth as ever, and I sighed loudly at the sound of it. Something simply about hearing my name from him was enough to send a chill through me and calm my nerves, dimming only some of the anger, but it was enough for now.

"Cade," I answered. "We speak again."

"You can't stay away, can you?" There was silence when I tried to gather my thoughts. "Angel? Are you okay?"

I closed my eyes and sighed again. He had used that nickname in the note he left me and a couple of times when we went on our picnic slash messed-up date, and I never corrected him. Because he wasn't doing it to tease or out of malice but genuine endearment, and there was something so sweet about that, so I allowed it.

Anyone else and I'd kick their ass.

"Why do you ask?" I whispered, aware of the emotion bubbling in my voice but trying to ignore it.

"You sound different."

"I'm in the garage."

He huffed out a laugh, a single deep note. "No, I mean, your voice sounds different. What's going on? Are you okay?"

The last few words were tinted with an almost frantic edge, and something told me if I called him to my side, he'd be here in an instant and beat up anyone who had made me feel bad. Despite myself, I smiled. "Just got suspended."

"What? Why?"

I shrugged before remembering he couldn't see the gesture. "Got into a fight over my father."

"Oh." Cade's voice dropped again, filled with sorrow. "I'm sorry, angel."

"It's okay," but my following sigh said it was pretty far from okay. "I needed to ask you about my handcuffs."

"I put them in your living room."

"So you told me, but I couldn't find them, and as part of my suspension, I have to hand them in. Can you come over and help me look?"

It was a feeble excuse, and both of us knew it. Anger, guilt, and fear were swirling inside me in an explosive cocktail that left me drained and empty instead of revving me up. I called him for company, but as soon as I heard his voice, all I could think about was his hands on me. Cade drew me to him, and I can't remember a time I've ever needed a physical release as much as I do now.

Beyond the distraction he could offer was a need for companionship. I was tired of being alone and lonely, and while it was a cage of my own building, I was struggling to break it apart. While Cade may not be able to break me free, he sure as hell would make my self-imprisonment more bearable.

"Yeah, okay, I can do that..." he trailed off. "I'm

out on delivery at the moment. Got a dining table to drop off and an old one to pick up. I'll be over in a few hours."

"Okay. I'm not going anywhere."

There was mostly silence on the line, where all I could hear was the rumbling of the truck he was driving in the background.

"Angel?"

He breathed the word out, and I imagined him saying it against my ear as he lay on top of me. Warmth flushed between my legs, and I leaned my head back against the headrest on the seat, sighing into the darkness.

"Yeah?" I whispered.

"If you want company, all you have to do is ask, you know?"

I sighed again. "I know." What I didn't know was how this man I had just met could see straight through me. "I'll see you soon... not like I'm going anywhere."

We said our goodbyes, and I hung up, dropping the phone into my purse in the passenger seat. I'd managed to make a right mess of things all because I couldn't keep my temper under wraps. Too much had happened too quickly with the suspicious death of Officer Kim, then the anniversary of my father's death, then Torres' odd comments. I simply hadn't been able to hold myself together. I was still a rookie by the standard of the old-school guys around the precinct, and I was pushing too many buttons.

But it was the right thing to do. Why must it be so difficult to balance what was right with what everyone expected? Keeping the peace when I witnessed an injustice was never my strong suit, and I needed to work on being the bigger person to spare people's feelings. But this wasn't some high-school squabble, this was a man's *life*. And if my suspicions were correct, several lives.

If I wanted to remain on the force, I'd need to keep my head down and play by the rules for a while, a good long while, judging by how deep I'd managed to get myself into shit. Unfortunately, that meant letting my father down, as if it were possible to let him down any more than I already had. In three years, I'd failed to bring up any solid evidence that pointed the finger at someone for his murder. There was a ton of suspicious circumstantial evidence, but without the resources of the force, how much I could do was limited to what I could find on public records and who was willing to speak to me, which in this city was next to none. Flashing your badge did nothing but make people clam up or run, and unfortunately, over the years, I'd poked around too much, and now my face was too well known. Anyone who knew anything about the current ownership of buildings that used to be Dad's would run the moment they saw me or threaten to call my sergeant if I didn't leave.

Cade popped into my mind, and I wondered if it would be too much to ask him to do some snooping around for me.

Scoffing, I snatched up my purse and stepped out of the car, slammed the door harder than I had intended, and rubbed the roof of my car gently, apologizing to her.

Not only would it be too much, but it would be a ridiculous ask. Cade was sweet, funny, and sexy as fuck, and maybe there was something there.

But was I willing to ruin yet another personal relationship over this investigation?

How far was I willing to go?

I kicked an empty paint can, cursing when it went flying and knocked several others over, causing one hell of a racket and an equally annoying mess in the garage.

To the ends of the earth.

That's how far I'd go to bring the person, or people, who had killed my father to justice, and if no one believed me, then maybe I'd need to take justice into my own hands.

While I could talk a big game, the thought sent a shudder down my spine.

Could I take a life?

Stripping off my clothes as I wandered through my house, which felt bigger than usual despite the mess, I pulled on a T-shirt and a pair of sweats before collapsing face-first on the couch and groaned loudly into the cushion.

Forgive me, Dad, I'm not giving up on you.

I simply need to keep my head down for a while.

He wouldn't want me to ruin my life trying to avenge his.

CHAPTER
8

CADE

When Nikki answered the door, her skin was imprinted with a dappling as though someone had held her face against the carpet with their foot. I was about to ask when she rubbed her cheek, pulling away a loose thread and groaning, flushing with embarrassment, as I stifled a grin.

"Sorry, fell asleep on the couch."

Well, that answered that question. I was about ready to break some heads if someone had hurt her like that. The logic of who would have been in her house, stomping her face into the carpet, and for her to be so calm escaped me. All I felt was that all-consuming possessiveness that spiked my heart rate, ready to protect my mate.

My *mate?*

Correction, to protect Nikki, a woman I know.

She looked a mess, and I didn't know what to say, unable to help feeling a certain level of responsibility. Because I knew things about her father and her family that she didn't, and she was torturing herself trying to find out information I could get for her. It would involve going back to Hell and questioning her father. It also meant I'd be required to explain my extended absence to those who actually gave a damn about the place and, therefore, may not be able to return to Earth straightaway. But questioning a human in Hell about their life on Earth in order to use that information to *change* something on Earth—was a big *fuck no*. I'd be killed for that shit, and that wouldn't do anyone any good. They were dead, and they could no longer affect the lives of those who knew them. It would be a huge mess if we tried to change anything.

I imagine the Big Man upstairs might get involved if demons started doing that shit.

That would be something, wouldn't it? A demon vigilante, finding out who murdered those in Hell straight from the mouths of the victims and coming to Earth to take them down.

I don't think it worked that way.

But Nikki, I couldn't tell her any of this, not that it would have been much comfort if I did. I couldn't tell her that perhaps her father's death wasn't worth looking into and he wasn't the man she thought he was. I couldn't tell her that not only had she spent three years seeking justice for someone who didn't deserve it, but the reason I knew these things was because I was a goddamn *demon.*

So for now, rather than saying anything, I simply pulled her against me and tried not to take too much pleasure in how she sighed and melted into my touch. My chin rested neatly on her head as she cuddled against me, and once again, I was struck by the sheer innocence of the move, the same as when she had held my hand. I was a demon and didn't deserve treatment like this.

I fucked.

I fought.

I moved on.

But Nikki's arms were wrapped around my back, and her fingers gripped my T-shirt under my leather jacket as though I was there to rescue her.

Damn, I wish I was.

But demons don't rescue.

We're the bad guys and always will be.

Nothing I do can change that, and with a pang, I realized I shouldn't even be here. Because by getting close to Nikki now, wasn't I filling her with false hope for something that would never be? For something *I* could never be, no matter how much I didn't fit in Hell, no matter how long I stayed on Earth, I'd always be a demon.

But she was mine for now, and I was still yet to

claim her. The warmth of her against me was distracting, the sun at my back nothing compared to the heat that radiated from her. My desire to touch her went beyond a fuck. Although I was dying to bury my cock in her sweet cunt, I wanted to *feel* her, to watch her face as she came apart under my hands and tongue.

When she had called me, the need was heavy in her voice, hidden and tangled behind a whirlwind of emotions she couldn't express. Would taking her physically while she was in this state be any better than taking her when she was drunk? I'd had no qualms about that the other night, but that was before I knew what the weight of guilt felt like against my chest—an incredibly human and weak feeling.

Frank was right—I was too soft.

A growl rumbled through my chest, and I pulled her closer to me.

She chuckled, shifting a hand around and patting my chest. "Did you just growl?"

"Yes," I said through gritted teeth.

"Why?" She moved to pull away, and I held her tighter against me. She didn't fight but simply relaxed back into my hold, and I had to resist the urge to hold her tighter still, fully aware of how easily I could hurt her if I lost control of my strength.

"Because you're upset."

"Aw..." Her voice was muffled against my chest. "How sweet."

I chuckled. "I can't tell if you're being sarcastic or not."

She huffed out a laugh. "At this point, neither can I."

When she pulled away again, I let her, and she looked at me with such intensity I almost took her right there. I knew this visit wasn't entirely innocent, and her body burned hot against mine, as desperate for my touch as I was to touch her. Guilt and shame flared in my stomach, and I ignored it.

Keeping my secrets from humans was nothing new, so why should it matter this time?

Because it did matter.

Because *she* mattered.

Because I'd never really put two and two together that the people in Hell still have families and loved ones on Earth. Like humans eating meat, they know damn well where it comes from, but they can live in some sort of perpetual denial as long as they don't have to see the process. But now there's a connection from where I used to be to where I am now and where I wanted to be.

And it was *her.*

But it shouldn't be. I wished it wasn't.

If she needed my touch to forget as much as I did, then so be it. Because given another chance to take her, I wouldn't waste it, and I'd taste every inch of her.

Her breasts pushed against my chest, and I'm certain she was curving her back into our embrace to intentionally enhance the sensation.

She shouldn't play these games with me. She didn't know what beast she was stirring.

The growl started again, and I stifled it. When Nikki straightened, her hands lingered on my waist, brushing the waistband of my jeans under my T-shirt. My abs tensed as she dragged her fingers across my stomach before dropping her arms to her sides.

A muscle in my jaw twitched.

If she made a move, I wouldn't be able to say no.

"Shall we start looking?" She swept an arm behind her as she turned slightly, and I nodded, walking past her into her townhouse. On the way here, I'd passed some cops outside a nightclub, closed for the day, and managed to use the shadows, darkening my skin until I was almost invisible and pairing it with my natural speed to take their handcuffs. I'd studied them as I walked to Nikki's and hadn't seen any hint of a serial number or anything identifiable, so hopefully, if I dropped them in her living room, she'd never know I'd shattered and subsequently stolen her original ones. It didn't sound like she needed any more trouble at work.

I'd kept the pieces in a drawer next to my bed.

Here I was, becoming attached to inanimate objects as a reminder of someone or something.

Was I always this fucking sentimental? Or had Earth changed me?

"Where have you searched?" I asked.

Nikki shrugged. "Honestly, nowhere yet. I had intended to but fell asleep as soon as I hit the couch... guess I was more exhausted than I realized." She stretched, and at this point, I wasn't bothering to hide it when I checked her out. Her T-shirt lifted with her arms to expose a taut stomach, paler than the skin on her arms and without the freckles. She had an outie belly button, and for some reason, even that turned me on.

Damn, I was beyond the point of no return with this woman.

"Where did you leave them?"

Nikki opened her eyes after her stretch, and her cheeks flushed as I slowly dragged my gaze up her body before finally resting on her eyes. Taking a moment to answer, I pointed to the coffee table. "There, I think."

While she nodded, she didn't move, and we simply stared at each other. When she bit her bottom lip, I thought of her doing the same at the graveyard and drawing blood, and I made fists at my sides, trying to contain my desire. The sweet taste of her blood would only be made better if I followed it by lapping up her cum from her thighs.

Fuck!

Something in me stirred, my muscles shifting under my shoulders and back, and I studied her, mentally measuring the distance to the bedroom and how long it would take to grab and take her there. Seconds, if I did it at full speed.

Even that was too long.

I could take her on the couch.

Or on the floor.

Or against the wall.

My cock twitched.

If you let me, I'll destroy you.

She moved first and started shifting magazines from the table, and it was only after she stood and stared at me, hands on hips, that I realized I had been staring at her ass.

"Did I bring you here to help or to leer at me?"

"I'll leer, thanks."

She laughed. "Do you want a beer?"

"Yeah, thank you."

She moved away, and with little to no grace, I shoved my hand in my pocket, dug through the tissues I'd used to surround the cuffs and muffle the sound, and brought them out. Tossing them quietly under the coffee table onto the carpet, I then kicked over a stack of books and hoped my face didn't betray my guilt.

Although hiding handcuffs was the least of my repressed guilt at the moment.

Nikki's scent was driving me crazy, and my demon stirred within as her invisible pheromones wafted around the small townhouse. The entire place smelled like her. She must have lived here for a long time, the furniture worn in and showing every sign of love and wear. If I were less controlled, I could bury my face in her couch and inhale her scent, letting it rile me up until I was more demon than man, ready to take her and lay my claim.

Territorial doesn't even begin to describe demons when it comes to sex.

Nikki wanted me too. It was written all over her face and how she held herself. The subtle bend of her hips as she had opened a drawer under the kitchen island to withdraw some glasses, almost more delicately than was necessary, as though she was trying to enhance the curves of her thighs and ass while she went about even a mundane task. She didn't usually move like that. We hadn't known each other long, but I'd spent enough time with her to know her style, her gait, and her natural body language.

Whether she knew it or not, although I suspected she knew damn well what she was doing, Nikki was calling me to her.

And who was I to deny?

Demon.

I was a demon, and not only that, I was one of *the*

demons who tortured a man she loved and admired. How sick am I that I can even look her in the face, let alone consider touching her with what I had done? The fact it was my nature, and Murphy had what was coming to him after a lifetime of crime and dark decisions, did not ease my guilt, although I felt that it should.

The reason it didn't, I suspected, was bending over in front of me.

Who keeps their beer on the bottom shelf of the refrigerator like that? Did she keep everything in her house on a low level? If I lived here, would I be perpetually faced with seeing her bend over constantly, taunting me with the lines of her body and ass?

It didn't seem so bad, but right now, I was fighting an internal battle.

A battle between a conscience I didn't know I had and a demon who was determined to fuck.

And I no doubt who would win.

I wasn't really fighting it because *fuck,* she was gorgeous.

Nikki returned with the beers, and I took mine without taking my eyes off hers.

"Any luck?" she asked.

"Not yet," I replied. My voice was gravelly as the battle for control raged within me, and it took me a moment to realize she was asking if I had found the handcuffs, not if I had gotten lucky.

Taking a long swig of her beer, Nikki licked the moisture from her lips. When I returned my gaze to hers, she cleared her throat. "Cade," she whispered.

"Uh," was all I managed to get out. My throat was dry, my hand clamped so tight around the bottle that if I didn't get it under control, the glass would shatter in my hand.

Say something smooth, you fucking idiot. You're a demon, for fuck's sake.

My sexual prowess and ability to seduce I'd waved about with such arrogance the other night seemed to have vanished because things had now changed. Somehow I wanted her more than ever, but rather than being only a physical release, there was more to it. The stakes were higher and much more fucking complicated.

But the logical part of my mind that erred toward human nature, the part of me that made me almost an outcast in Hell, was being overridden by my demon. As Nikki stood in front of me, her tongue gliding across her lips reminding me of the way she'd mimicked that movement over my cock and the scent of her arousal thick in the air between us, I was losing what little hold I had on myself.

"It's probably obvious, but I didn't invite you over just to look for the handcuffs." Her gaze swept the mess on the living room floor before returning to my eyes. "Although we can resume that. Later." She lifted a hand to place a palm on my chest. "I think you and I have unfinished business, and I'd be lying if I said I hadn't been thinking about it."

On instinct, I swiped out, grasping her wrist the second she made contact with the fabric of my T-shirt. Her eyes widened, and where I expected to see fear at the speed with which I had moved, I saw lust flare there, burning desire screaming out to be taken.

By me.

My shoulders tensed as my muscles rippled, my demon stirring at the scent of her arousal and skin. I bet she'd taste so fucking sweet on my tongue.

"I'm gonna need you to say it, Cade," she whispered, throwing the words back at me that I had used on her the night we met. "Then later, you can *beg* me."

She was strong, and I was used to women who fell at my feet responding to my presence or the hints of my demon I let peek through the surface that had human men and women alike craving release or simply because they wanted to be dominated and ravished. But Nikki, she had handcuffed me to her fucking bed the first chance she got.

I needed to show her who was the boss.

Putting my drink down, I then used the same speed to grab her other wrist and guided her until she released her drink and set it on the coffee table. A shudder ran down her spine, and she trembled in my touch as I held her arms behind her back, maneuvered until I could comfortably hold both her hands in mine, and then dragged a finger down her cheek, tracing over her lips that trembled slightly, and down her neck. My heart pounded in my chest, and I could almost see the blood pulsing through her veins.

Drink her. Drain her.

No. I can't.

I couldn't help lowering my face to her neck, dragging in a deep breath, and running my teeth along her throat's delicate tendons and lines. Nikki shuddered again, and I felt the vibrations of her moan across my lips as I kissed her collarbone.

"Yes," I whispered against her skin. "I'll claim you."

"That's not what I meant—"

Silencing her with a kiss, I thrust my tongue into her mouth, groaned with her as she moaned and sucked on my tongue, and fought for control. It was a fight she was losing. Although she squirmed against my grip on her hands, my fingers stayed closed in a vice-like grip around her.

She was mine to command, to control, to *fuck.*

She was *mine.*

CHAPTER
9

NIKKI

God.

This man, his touch, his body, everything about him was unbelievable.

The way I was behaving wasn't me. I wasn't a woman to lie back and simply let the man do everything, but I was coming undone under his fingers, and every time I tried to move and take back some control, he'd hold me still, his grip tightening around my hands and wrists.

And let's be honest, I wasn't fighting that hard.

Because I didn't want to think right now, and Cade was *very* good at making me forget everything outside his wandering fingers and tongue. Cade was stronger than I'd anticipated. His body was lean but sculpted, and I should've realized his strength simply by looking at him. But he took control of my mind and body easily, and I might as well be limp in his arms with the way he played with my senses.

This wasn't how things were supposed to be. We were supposed to have a delicious back-and-forth that lasted days or weeks. We were meant to have moments of *oops, our hands touched* and staring into each other's eyes longingly over a shared milkshake. We were not meant to start off with a funeral, a failed one-night stand, me unconscious, and a missing pair of handcuffs.

Yet I was here, and right now I wanted more than anything else to simply touch him. I needed to run my palms over his chest, trace the outline of his muscles with my fingers, dip my fingertips under the waistband of his jeans, and tease my nails up the length of his cock.

But I wasn't even getting that because he had my hands held together in only one of his while he played my body with his kisses and fingers. I gasped as he slipped his hand underneath my T-shirt, and when he cupped my breast in his palm, he growled against my neck.

Growling, I've never had a man *growl* at me before like that.

Fuck, it was hot.

I wanted the same thing now that I did after Kim's funeral—to forget for a while. The more Cade touched me, the more his fingers ignited passion against my skin, but it was much more than that. He expertly palmed my breast before he snuck his fingers up under my bra and pinched my nipple. I moaned into his mouth. He hadn't stopped kissing me, playing his tongue against mine with the same fervor as his hand explored my body.

If he was trying to claim me, then I was going to let him.

His grip on my hands behind my back eased when I relaxed against him, but still held, as though he was ready for me to start fighting him again. But I wouldn't, not this time at least. I was his to use as he pleased because I had no doubt even if he fucked me like a fucktoy, he wouldn't rest until I had the same pleasure he did.

I tried not to think about the level of trust it took for me to let go, even this much.

Because this wasn't a time for thinking.

We broke away from each other, and Cade shrugged out of his jacket, letting it fall to the floor behind him. Lifting his T-shirt over his head, I followed the edge of the fabric as it revealed more of him to me.

Fuck.

Immediately, I placed my hands on his chest and pressed my body against his, desperate to feel the hard lines of him against me. Hell, something was definitely hard. His erection was pressed against his jeans, and when I moved next to him, he wrapped his arms around me, trapped my hands between us, and ground his crotch against mine. Fire ignited between my legs with every rub of his shaft against my clit. Even through our clothes, he moved with a rhythm and force that had me practically keening for more. Christ, if he could almost make me peak from a dry hump, how fucking good would it be to feel him *inside* me, driving away with that same rhythm?

I didn't want to wait any longer.

Squirming against his hold, I managed to get my hands low enough to undo his belt and begin working at the button and fly on his jeans. Cade stopped me only long enough to pull my T-shirt over my head and unlatch my bra, sliding it down my arms.

Foreplay could wait until next time because the heat burning inside me was almost too much to bear.

"Cade..." I panted out, my fingers fumbling, "... just fuck me already, *please.*"

Something passed across his eyes, his expression darkened, and a trick of the light made his eyes appear yellow for a moment. Wild. When I glanced behind me for the source of the illusion, I squealed when Cade lifted me over his shoulder and carried me toward the bedroom at the rear of the house.

With glee, I reached up and managed to tap my fingers against the light fitting I was forever trying to touch, and I released a delighted giggle. This earned me a slap against my ass from Cade, followed by another growl when I screamed out, more in shock than pain.

Bouncing as Cade dropped me against the mattress, he fought with my sweatpants as he tugged them down over my legs. "What are you giggling at?" he asked, his voice was deep, almost not his own, and the muscles in his jaw were tense. He wasn't looking at my face, his eyes instead hungrily swept over my body when I lay naked in front of him.

"I was just..." My words faded into nothing as he finished undressing in front of me.

Holy. Shit.

"Uh..." I said. I knew I shouldn't stare, but I couldn't tear my gaze away from his cock.

He glanced down, his grin edging with smugness when he looked back at me. "Is there a problem, angel?"

"Cade, I..." I swallowed, and he frowned as I attempted to cover my body with my hands. Suddenly, the cool air against my skin was too much after the heat I had felt from him earlier, and I was abruptly reminded of how long it had been since I'd had someone in my bedroom. I didn't realize the extent of my obsession with work and my investigation until a friend of mine, Catherine, contacted me, saying she hadn't seen me in over a year and missed me.

Over a year, had it really been that long?

Because the last time I went out with the girls was the last time I got any.

The heat rose in my cheeks, and I couldn't stop it. I pulled my gaze away from the fucking monster between his legs and looked into his eyes. Was I really that drunk the other night that I didn't remember how fucking big he was? I'd had that thing in my mouth. Was I blind to the fact I'd barely have been swallowing the head with how my lips stretched around him?

The smug grin had gone and was replaced with concern, although his jaw was still tense.

I'd broken the mood.

I sat up and shifted toward the head of the bed. "It's um…" Another look at his cock, another muttered curse. "It's been a while."

"Do you not want to…" The confusion was evident in both his tone and how his brow furrowed.

Fuck, I was blowing this.

"No, I do, I really fucking do. It's just… fuck!" *I really couldn't help staring at his cock.* "What if it doesn't… fit?"

"What happened to the woman who handcuffed me to the bed and practically shouted *yee-haw?*"

The way he looked at me had me shuddering, and that dark expression passed over his face again. It's how I imagined a wolf would look at its prey. I stayed still as Cade kneeled on the bed before crawling toward me. I'd like to say I held his eye contact, but my gaze kept drifting between his legs. I wanted to reach out and touch the tip. Cade took my hands and pulled them from covering my body, exposing me to him once again. His smile was deadly as he guided me to lay down and braced himself over me, his breath warm against my neck as he began rubbing the length of his cock against my thigh.

"It'll fit just fine." It was a promise.

Fuck.

He rocked against me, and I whimpered, trailing my hands up his arms, taking in the delicious definition of his muscles and moving up until I was clasping his back. My thighs were wet by the time he shifted, so his shaft was between my pussy lips and rubbed against my clit. *God.* I moaned and moved against him, and when he whispered in my ear, it almost pushed me over the edge.

"That's it, angel... get nice and wet for me." He hummed, pressing harder, his thrusts becoming slower but longer against me, drawing out the sensation. "Fuck, you feel so good. Get that pussy soaking before I fuck you."

"Oh God," the words were barely a whisper past my lips. He mumbled something, and I didn't catch it, too lost in the building pleasure. "What?"

"Condom?" he asked.

When he moved to lift his body from mine and ceased his thrusting against my clit, I moaned and cried out his name. When did I get so needy? But I couldn't help it, any hesitation I had was gone, and all I wanted was to feel the incredible stretch his cock would bring.

Bareback.

I was on birth control, and while that wasn't the only consideration, I simply didn't want any barriers between Cade and me. Foolish, maybe, but everywhere he touched me felt like fire, and I was panting, so close to release yet again simply from his rubbing against me.

"Just fucking fuck me," I said through gritted teeth. "Now... *please.*"

I thought for a moment he was going to argue, but he simply growled again and allowed me to pull him down on top of me. Positioning himself between my thighs, he reached down and guided the head of his cock until it pressed against my entrance.

I let fly a string of curses and praises as he penetrated me, thankful that despite how wet I was, he took his time, moving in one smooth motion until he was finally fully sheathed within me. Cade was frowning, his eyes clamped closed as he braced himself above me, his arms trembling with the effort of taking it slow. He almost lost control when he was nearly fully in, finishing off with a final hard thrust that had me crying out.

Panting together, we stayed still for a moment.

"Are you okay?" he whispered.

"Yes."

"I can't promise I'll be gentle if you keep doing that," he said.

"Doing what?"

"Clenching around me."

At his words, I clenched again, unaware I had been doing it before, and he growled, low and deep. The muscles in his arms were tense next to my head, and he leaned on his elbows. I didn't think he'd take me like this, picturing him more a bend-over-and-fuck kind of guy. But I liked him on top of me where I could watch his body. Every motion, every tense and release of his muscles as he began rocking against me. That slow, incredible rhythm of his made me wish I were watching from the other side of the room, taking in the gyration of his hips until I went crazy with lust. As a flush of warmth flooded my already wet pussy at the thought, I moaned, not wanting to be anywhere but under him. The slick drag of cock inside me was nothing short of magic, and I cried out every time Cade pushed fully in. His hands gripped the sheets, bunching the fabric up under his fingers, and I realized how hard he was trying to take it slow, allowing me to adjust to his size.

It felt amazing.

Until it wasn't enough.

"More…" I whispered.

Cade opened his eyes, watching my face as he pulled almost all the way out before slamming hard into me. I cried out a strangled "Yes," and something in him changed.

He became more animal than human.

Cade gripped my hips, and he fucking unleashed on me. Whatever I was expecting from him, this man who seemed so sweet, funny, and relaxed, it wasn't to be fucked within an inch of my life. A growl resonated from his chest as his grip on me increased, pounding into me mercilessly. My body accommodated him, and every inch of him was sweet pleasure and stretch. When I moved to grip his arms, he pulled out, leaving me feeling empty before he flipped me over.

"Cade…"

He pressed his hand to my head, shoving my cheek into the pillow before leaning over me. He dragged his cock back and forth over my clit again, and I moaned, grinding against him. "Grip the pillows if you have to, angel, but keep your head and hands down, or I'll have to punish you."

I wiggled my ass against him, enticing another growl that made me smirk.

What if I wanted to be punished?

As though reading my thoughts, his hand snaked around my throat, his voice low and dangerous next to my ear. "I didn't hear a response from you."

"Yes..."

"Yes, *what?*"

My jaw tensed as I grit my teeth, and he chuckled. One hand stayed on my throat, and when the other moved between my legs, he pinched my clit gently between his fingers, rolling the sensitive bud until I was jerking underneath him.

"Yes?" he prompted, his voice still a dangerous whisper against me.

This wasn't at all what I expected from Cade—the man he was in bed was a darker version of him. I didn't feel unsafe, but fuck, he felt *dangerous.* His threats for punishment were real and, with them, the promise of absolute pleasure. But I wasn't going to submit that easily. Although every nerve in my body was screaming at me to simply say the word and let him be the boss, it wasn't my nature to do so. I was no BDSM Dom by any stretch, but I liked to take control, to ride a man while holding his wrists against the headboard, watching his head loll and eyes screw shut as I fucked his brains out.

Cade was claiming that control back from me.

God, part of me wanted him to use me.

A big part of me.

Who was I kidding? Almost all of me, except this remaining stubborn streak, not willing to give in without a fight.

I whimpered as he continued his assault on my

clit, his cock's hard length sliding against my leg as he continued slow thrusts. Cade kissed and nipped at my neck, the gentle ministrations thrown off by his grip on my throat. My climax was building, but I'd dug myself into a hole now, and with each second that passed, letting go of that thread of control that remained was getting harder. The problem was I was no good at admitting I was wrong. I could feel his lips against my neck, smiling, feeling my internal battle. My lips pressed together to keep the word *sir* from slipping past, but my hips ground against the air, wanting more.

He slipped a finger inside me, and I moaned against the pillow.

"It's not enough for you, is it, angel?" Cade muttered. "You don't want my fingers, you need my cock, stretching you, claiming you." He pumped his finger in my pussy a few times, the room filling with the obscene sounds of arousal I couldn't hide, no matter how stubborn I wanted to be.

"Please," I begged him for the release that was right there as his fingers returned to my clit, practically throbbing with the need to come. Cade's fingers tightened around my throat, and I gasped.

"Please, *what?*"

Gritting my teeth, I whimpered before moaning again as another jolt of pleasure coursed through me.

Fuck you, Cade.

"Please…" I panted, "… *sir.*"

He growled his approval, doubling the speed of his efforts against my clit. "Good girl."

I couldn't help it. The moans escaping my lips were increasing in pitch, and I was so close. *So close.*

He penetrated me from behind in one motion, his fingers still working my clit in small, tight circles, and as I came, I tightened around his cock, forcing him to push past the resistance and open me up to him. Cade continued a gentle rhythm of thrusts as I shuddered and twitched around his cock, riding out the waves of my orgasm.

"Are you ready to be fucked, angel?"

I simply moaned in response, and this time when he leaned over me, his cock hit a new angle, rubbing against my G-spot. He brushed my hair from my face before grabbing a handful and hissing in my ear. "I asked you a question."

"Yes, sir. I'm ready to be fucked." I panted out, and he seemed satisfied, returning to kneel behind me and gripping my hips as he increased speed, slowly this time, building with each thrust until the headboard was banging against the wall. Gripping the sheets, I moaned loudly into the pillow. *Fuck, did this guy have stamina or what?* I could barely breathe, my breath hitching with each thrust as I cried out every time he pushed in. Cade's grip on my hips became almost painful, and he reached between my legs again, flicking his finger over my clit and making me jolt.

"Come again."

"Cade..."

"Come. I want to feel you squeeze my cock when I spill inside you."

"Oh God..."

Like I had much choice. His fingers worked me expertly, and the moment before release shuddered through me, he pinched my clit harshly, then I exploded with pleasure and sensation. Cade roared as he came and didn't stop rubbing my clit until his thrusts slowed and stopped.

Bent over me, Cade rested his cheek between my shoulder blades, his fingers flexing on my hips and cock twitching within me, still hard. Slowly, he pulled from me before collapsing on the bed and pulling my body against his, my back hitting his chest as he curled around me.

After a moment, he asked. "Did I hurt you?"

"No," I whispered. "That was amazing."

He chuckled. "You don't like letting go of control, do you?"

Playfully, I swatted his arm as it lay across my stomach. "You can talk."

His lips curved into a smile against my shoulder before he took a deep breath, burying himself against me. I was hypersensitive to every hard line of his body, and for the first time in a long time, I truly relaxed.

CHAPTER 10

CADE

Nikki had disappeared into the bathroom, and I lay sprawled on her bed, my hands tucked behind my head as I stared at the ceiling. She had been everything I craved and more, her tight pussy stretching around me, taking every fucking inch. My cock twitched against my leg as I replayed the entire scene in my head. Looks like I'd met my match.

There was a satisfied humming drifting from the bathroom, an unrecognizable tune as the tap ran freely, water splashing into the porcelain sink. Rolling my head to the side, the handcuffs' key glinted in the light from the window and caught my eye.

Fuck.

The *key!*

I didn't think to grab the key when I'd stolen the replacement cuffs.

Oh shit.

Nikki was practically bouncing as she emerged from the bathroom, that slight pink flush on her cheeks enunciating the freckles against her otherwise pale skin. She looked even more like an angel with her hair around her shoulders and her naked body lit up in the sunlight, her pale nipples alert above a smattering of goose bumps as the cooling air moved across her skin.

My cock twitched again.

I'd *need* her again soon.

I *wanted* her right now.

"Shall we get back to searching?" she asked.

"*Back to* implies we started in the first place."

"Weren't you looking while I got us drinks?"

I watched her as she sat on the edge of the bed, folding one leg neatly under the other. "Maybe," I said, allowing myself a leisurely gaze over her body, "... or maybe I was watching your ass."

She smirked. "Well, watch my ass as I get dressed, then come help me look."

Lifting myself into a sitting position, I did exactly that, and memorized the lines of her body as she pulled on some clothes she had lying around, her others having been discarded in the living room earlier. The black tank and baggy three-quarter shorts did nothing to dim how hot she was. I knew what she looked like under those clothes now, and the image of her writhing underneath me, her lips pouted, and a small frown as she adjusted to my size was forever imprinted in my mind.

Sighing, I rolled off the bed and pulled my pants back on, not bothering with anything else. Something told me it wouldn't be long before I'd be taking them off again. I followed her back down the hall into the living room, where Nikki immediately bent over to adjust a pile of books.

I couldn't help myself.

Approaching, I grabbed her hips as she bent at the waist, her ass in the air. Pushing against her, I knew she'd be able to feel my cock through our clothes, and she moaned and wiggled as I ground against her, rubbing my cock along her pussy and between her ass cheeks. When she stood, her cheeks were flushed, and she grinned at me, dragging her teeth across her lip.

"Well…" I said, flexing my fingers on her hips, "… aren't we going to search for the cuffs?"

She glared at me, unsure what game I was playing. When she bent again, I slid my hand down the back of her shorts, and she giggled until I cupped her cheek in my palm and pushed my middle finger into her ass. Nikki jumped away from me like a shot, and if possible, her cheeks were even redder. "You're not going to find them in there!"

My lips lifted into a smirk. Her eyes were wide,

but it wasn't anger I saw there.

Arousal and curiosity.

Good to know. Store that information for later.

Nikki stared at me for a moment, and I waited for her to protest further. But she closed the gap between us, and when I snaked my arms around her waist, she didn't stop me. She was so warm against me, a little fireball, and she ignited every part of me. A strangled cry was torn from me when she gripped my cock through my pants. Hard.

"You ready to help?" She smirked at me.

"Yeah," I choked out.

Nikki's grip tightened, and I gritted my teeth, the pain so sweet. "Yes, *what?*" she crooned.

Oh, *fuck no.*

My hand was around her throat, and she sucked air in sharply as I tightened my grip. My other hand grabbed her wrist until she was forced to release her grip on me, which had increased. "That's not going to work on me, angel," I said, a growl I couldn't control rumbling deep in my chest. "I'm the boss in that department."

Her eyes flashed with disobedience, and she grinned. "We'll see about that."

Letting her go, we stared at each other for a moment longer, the challenge I had laid out hung heavy in the air between us. I debated if I should throw her over my lap and spank her or toss her over the couch and fuck her again. Then she bent, slowly and purposefully, turning back and smirking when she saw my gaze on her ass as if I had any chance of resisting. My cock twitched, but she began making a new pile of books next to the fireplace, moving and grabbing books and magazines from around the room systematically.

Steering clear of where I planted the stolen cuffs, I followed suit. Fear began to tug at my chest as I kneeled next to the couch, stacking up papers that were on the small table, covering the base of a lamp that looked to be antique but may have simply been designed to appear that way. I followed Nikki's lead and built a pile of files next to the fireplace, my curiosity getting the better of me as the pile increased. Everything I pulled from the table, the couch, and under the couch was the same—folders full of notes and photographs, dodgy pictures that were so blurred and skewed they must've been copies of copies, and Post-it notes with questions scrawled across them.

It took me longer than it should have, distracted by my selfish thoughts of waiting to be caught out for bringing back the wrong handcuffs to realize these were Nikki's investigations into her father's death. I began to skim-read a few as I gathered them, aware that I was probably crossing a line into what was acceptable prying but unable to stop myself.

She'd followed the money—always a good start.

But the ownership of the buildings which were once her father's had changed and became complicated, being switched between private businesses, trusts, and names of people who didn't exist, until she was going around in circles and ending up nowhere. Images of the buildings she either knew or suspected to have been her father's were surrounded by notes in her scrawled writing, every slanted letter joined to the next and barely a space between words. It looked like no one was willing to talk to her, whether she tried to use her uniform to get through the door or not.

A file was snatched from my hand, and I looked up to meet her eyes, expecting to see anger but instead finding embarrassment and shame.

"I'm taking a break from investigating," Nikki said, turning away from me.

Thank God. "Why's that?"

Nikki sighed, adding the file to the stack I had already created. "I don't think he'd want me to wile my life away trying to find his killer." Before I could respond, she'd spun around to face me, her cheeks flaming again. "But I'm not giving up, not now, not ever. I'll let things settle down at work, make them *think* I've stopped, and then I'll keep going." Her gaze dropped to the floor, and her jaw worked as she tensed and released like she was grinding her teeth. "I won't give up on him."

She was never going to stop.

As though I didn't know that already, she had already proven herself to me as stubborn and headstrong. If she wasn't willing to relinquish the smallest amount of control with me, how far would she go to avenge someone she loved? To the ends of the earth and until her last breath, I imagined she wouldn't stop searching.

I had to help if only to ease her mind so she could move on.

But I couldn't tell her what I knew. I'd had to find some other way to help.

Maybe if I could solve it *for* her.

"Aha!"

I was snapped back to reality as Nikki straightened, holding the handcuffs I had planted under the coffee table. She strolled to the bedroom and came back with the key, and I held my breath as she pressed the key into the cuff and sighed as it clicked and released.

A universal key.

Or specific by police station, perhaps.

Either way, I'd gotten away with it.

Barely.

"So what happens now?" I asked, leaning against the back of the couch.

She glanced at the cheap plastic clock on the wall. "Tomorrow I'll go drop them at the station, and then... sit on my ass for four weeks."

My demon stirred. "You could sit on my face if

you prefer."

Nikki's skin flushed, and her mouth dropped open at my words. I couldn't help it. Despite the conflicting emotions that stirred in me, I'd had her now, and I knew I'd never get enough of her. My guilt was easy to quash when faced with her so long as I didn't look too deeply into her eyes and the pain that was constantly there—pain which she blamed herself for. She wasn't responsible for the person her father was. He met his death because of his own doing, I was certain of it. Nikki was too loyal for her own good.

But all of this I could push to the side because she was fucking incredible, and her touch burned against me like no other had before. I loved her defiance, her humor, and simply her company. I'd had her body once, and it would never be enough now.

Already my length was straining against my pants, and I stalked toward her, backing her against the stone of the fireplace and leaning in until my lips were next to her neck, breathing in the scent of her. Nikki shuddered, and the scent of her arousal flooded the air between us, settling around me like embers ready to ignite me again, and my senses spiked.

"Got any plans tonight?" I whispered.

I shouldn't do this. I should stay far away from Nikki, help her, and then let her move on with her life. As it were, I was a constant threat, not only because of my demon but because I'd forever be watching what I say and do, not wanting to let slip any of the secrets I knew about her family.

Not to mention the secret about what *I* was.

But she was intoxicating in the best of ways, and the guilt combined with how I felt in her presence was creating a storm that raged within me. No matter how hard I fucked her, I couldn't fuck away the guilt.

Her lips found mine as she placed her palm on my cheek, and I opened my mouth to let her tongue dance against mine, moaning into the sensation of her taste—sweet and salty perfection. I wanted her to be rough. I *needed* her to treat me like a one-night stand and demand that this could never be anything more than that. But her touch was soft and delicate, her tongue massaging mine, exploring my mouth as she hummed with contentment, all previous aggravation and defiance forgotten—for now, at least. I'd be challenging her unwillingness to let go of control soon enough.

"No plans," she said, pulling away from the kiss barely enough to answer.

My instinct and body were winning, and I was losing the will to fight the battle against this desire.

Because whatever I was, however much I didn't fit in with the other demons or how much I learned on Earth and changed the longer I was here, I was still a demon, and my demon still controlled me as much as I did it.

Why should I fight it? Why couldn't I have what I wanted? Her world and mine were filled with examples of beings taking what they wanted without regard for anything else. Why couldn't I be one of them?

And it was her—all I wanted was *her.*

A growl emanated deep in my throat, and I grabbed her ass, instinctively grinding against her as she wrapped a leg around my thigh.

"You have plans now," I muttered, and she chuckled.

The mood changed, and it was with desperation that she kissed me, grabbing my face and winding one arm around my neck, pulling me against her as I gripped her ass harder, moving my hand only enough to shove it down under the elastic of her waistband to feel flesh against my palm. I'm sure the reminder of her dad's case was playing on her mind as much as it was mine.

Would there ever be a right time to tell her what I was?

I should leave now before I get in too deep.

It was already too late for that.

"Watch those fingers, buster," she warned, and I chuckled. I traced my fingers delicately around the soft area of skin where her pubic hair started, soft blonde hairs that would tickle my nose when I fucked her hot cunt with my tongue. Nikki squirmed under my touch as I traced my fingers around, under the inviting curve of her ass, and tempted her hole.

"You liked it," I said, and she squirmed before I moved my hand away.

Her cheeks flushed again, and she covered it by burying her face in the crook of my neck before kissing and nipping at my shoulder. "Take me, Cade," she whispered, her breathing coming in pants. "Please."

She didn't have to ask twice.

After I talked my way past the receptionist, I strolled through the hallway lined with glass walls and doors for various offices and meeting rooms, throwing around the opulence of the office and sending exactly the message I imagined it intended to—*we can afford this place, and you can only* dream *of being here.* Feeling as out of place as I looked, I shoved my hands into my jacket pocket.

As I turned the corner directed by the girl at reception, I faced the wide foyer that led to Frank's expansive office. Frank was leaning against his personal secretary's desk, his shirt sleeves rolled up exposing his arms, the turned-up fabric barely holding together as he flexed. The secretary couldn't keep her eyes on his, her gaze slipping away from his face to sweep over his body before she'd realize what she was doing and look at his face again. The pen she nervously tapped against the piles of forgotten paperwork on her desk never stopped, and I chuckled. Watching her falling under the spell was amusing. Can't say I'd seen it from the outside before.

She let out a squeak of a sound upon seeing me and pushed herself away from Frank, flushing furiously as she began typing while Frank stood smirking.

"Couldn't stay away, I see. Did you come about the job offer?" Frank said.

I scoffed, smiling as we slapped each other on the back—no hard feelings, even after tearing each other apart the other night. Demons will be demons, and the release was good for us. After a final and particularly rough slap on my shoulder, I grunted as Frank chuckled and reminded myself to get some workouts in. I wanted to give him a run for his money next time.

"Hardly," I said, resisting the urge to rub my shoulder. "Actually, I came to ask a favor."

Frank rolled his eyes, an exaggerated motion which he ended in a wink directed toward his secretary, who flushed again and turned away when she saw me observing the exchange.

"Come into my office."

The office was sparsely furnished with only the large desk near the window, Frank's chair, and one for a visitor. Otherwise, the remainder of the space was unused. There were boxes around, and I imagined he and Mike were still settling into the larger office. It wouldn't take long for him to make it his own, claiming his territory.

He'd already started claiming his space by having the chair that resides behind the large desk much wider and taller than the guest chair.

"Nice throne," I commented as I sat on the smaller chair. I figured starting a fight with Frank right before asking him for something wouldn't be the best move. Although, with his smug-fucking-face, it was tempting. He watched as my gaze took in the office and the view from the large window, and his face simply screamed his pride and his love of rubbing his success into the face of any visitor to his domain. Yeah, he was destined for this sort of role, ready to put the work in and more ready to gloat about his success. Flinging my feet up, I rested them on the desk as I leaned back, the chair squeaking its protest. As Frank passed me, he shoved my feet from his desk, adding a swift punch to the shoulder before sitting opposite me, purposefully lifting his feet and bringing them to rest on the desk in the same position he had denied me.

He grinned as I scowled. Arrogant prick.

Glancing back at the secretary, whose face had returned to an almost normal color instead of the crimson blush that made her skin almost match her hair tone, I asked Frank, "Fucked her yet?"

He smirked. "Not yet, but I will. She's only a temp while Abigail is on leave."

"Have you fucked Abigail too?"

Frank's resulting laugh was loud and booming. "No. She thinks she's old enough to be my grandmother." My turn to laugh. If only she knew. "You didn't come here to talk about my sex life."

Sighing, I leaned back in my chair as it squeaked again under my weight. For a moment, I was tempted to rock back and forth in it, see how much I could make it squeak before Frank's jaw twitched with irritation.

Again, not the time to be antagonizing the older demon.

"No, I came to ask a favor."

"So you said. What's wrong? You needed me to fight, and now you need me to fuck your woman too?" The growl that escaped my throat was involuntary, and Frank didn't bother to hide the delight on his face. "Oh! Still feeling a bit territorial, are we?"

"It'll pass," I lied, despite taking Nikki three more

times yesterday and well into the night, my system still wasn't satiated, and I was starting to fear it was less about controlling my demon and more about the protective and possessive desire I had for her, specifically. "Look, she's throwing her life away investigating the murder of her father—"

"What's it to you?"

I debated how much to tell him, and Frank simply arched a dark eyebrow at me, waiting. "He's not worth avenging," I said lamely.

"If you're going to come in here and ask me for favors, you better be willing to give me more than that, Cade. We may be blood, but that doesn't mean much for demons, and you know that."

"Fine." I took a breath, wondering how much he needed to know so he'd help me. "She seems to think he was some upstanding businessman because, for whatever reason, he treated her like a princess and was a stand-up father. But he was a corrupt, murdering criminal who ran half the shit at the other end of this city, mostly drugs, but there was some murder-for-hire shit in there. He certainly had no qualms about killing to get what he needed. She's determined to find out who murdered him, and I can either help her along or watch her waste her life away."

"I'll ask again, what's it to you what she does with her life? How do you even know who her father was?"

"I saw a photo…" I spat out, gritting my teeth, "… and I recognized him from Hell. He was one of mine."

Frank leaned back in his seat. "Ah." I waited for some nugget of wisdom from the eldest of our brothers, but he said nothing more until, "What do you need from me?"

"You've been here a while. I want someone I can talk to who can give me information she won't be able to find. Maybe if I can find her brother, he'll know something. She said she hasn't spoken to him since her dad died. Or even better, if I can just find out who did it and some evidence, then point the cops toward them and end this."

Frank chuckled, slid his feet from his desk, and leaned forward again, watching me as he rested his chin on his fingers. "You know solving crimes isn't what demons do, right?"

"Pretty sure they don't become CEOs either."

"Touché. But then again, you never really did fit in back home, did you, *parvulus puer*?"

"Don't call me that."

Frank's lip lifted into something between a smirk and a sneer. The nickname sounded cute, but for us it was far from endearing—the term *little boy* was intended to offend. Beyond the difference between us in years, I was often at the receiving end of insults due to never quite holding the pleasure-for-violence streak that was pivotal to so many demons.

And worse than insults.

Never by Frank, he'd tease, but he wasn't the type to outright bully, not unless you seriously pissed him off. But demon siblings were hardly compassionate with one another, and everyone was left to fight their own battles.

"All right, I think I know someone you can talk to," Frank said.

"Wh—"

"But," Frank held a finger out, making sure I was holding his eye contact. I bared my teeth at him, not needing to be treated like a child. "You watch out for this guy, okay? He's older than me and absolutely can not be trusted. I can keep him under control because I have money to satiate him and keep him mostly from trouble, and physically, I'm stronger than he is and can shake him up a bit. But I have no doubt he's got his slimy fingers in everything he can get into to make extra cash. He likes to gamble and fuck, but he doesn't fit in... humans simply don't trust him. He can't seem to blend in like you or I. He's too dark inside."

That was concerning, but I didn't let it show on my face. "I can take care of myself—"

"Watch yourself around him. I fucking mean it, Cade."

"All right, I got it, Frank."

Frank stared at me for a moment longer, his dark

curls falling over his forehead as he leaned forward to stare intently, probably an intimidation technique, and I'd never admit to him it was almost working. He sighed, then said, "For a handful of cash, he'll tell you what he knows, but do *not* tell him I sent you to him. I'll never hear the end of it, and he'll think he has the upper hand on me. One day I'm going to cut him loose, but for now, it's a matter of keep-your-enemies-closer type deal. I've no doubt he's in with every dodgy fucker he can get in with, so he may know something or someone who does."

"Thank you."

"Don't thank me. I'm not thrilled about you crossing his path. But if it'll help ease your conscience about this woman, then so be it."

"Who said I was feeling guilty?"

Frank's lip twitched. "It's written all over your face, *parvulus puer.* You never were a good liar."

My stomach felt like lead within me. I didn't want to have to lie to Nikki beyond the obvious of keeping my identity hidden. But holding this back from her wasn't sitting well with me. I wished we could investigate together and I could be pivotal in her solving this crime so she could finally rest. Maybe it was slightly childish, but I wanted to be the center of her attention.

I wanted to help, then maybe Nikki could rest without ever having to know the truth about who

Murphy really was.

Who was I to sully her memories with something as horrid as reality?

CHAPTER
11

NIKKI

Cade woke me before he left in the morning. Although I managed to drag him back into bed, clutching onto his arms and pulling him on top of me, he'd rewarded my desire with a heated make-out session full of promises before he pulled away and told me he had to run some errands.

What errands could be more important than his mouth between my legs?

Or mine between his.

Fuck. He was so *fucking hot!*

I felt giddy, like a goddamn teenager or something, a raging bag of hormones that piqued whenever he touched me. I'm not sure what I expected from him, but it certainly wasn't the animalistic fucking he gave when he finally let go. Cade had been so gentle, well, mostly with his kisses and caresses, but once that barrier was down, there was a darkness behind his eyes. He'd watch me as though I were a possession, as though he owned me.

And I'd be lying if I said I didn't love it.

But that didn't mean I wouldn't fight him for power between the sheets.

Despite everything going on, my suspension wasn't far from the front of my mind, and as always, thoughts of my father's case pretty much consumed every part of my brain not dedicated to eating and breathing. But I was feeling pretty good. There was a spring in my step and an unmistakable sweet ache between my thighs, all thanks to Cade.

A shiver ran down my spine, and simply thinking of him touching me was enough to get me in the mood again. I wondered if he had planned to come back and see me after his *errands* and if it would be too much to call him and ask.

Picking up my cell, I released a low whistle. It was almost ten, I'd slept in after Cade had left, and apparently, I needed the sleep. A bubble of resentment sprung up in my gut, and I recognized it for what it was a second before I was overcome with guilt for allowing it to exist in the first place. Resentment for my father's case, for both my inability to solve it and the fact it had taken over my life. I hadn't seen my girlfriends in a year, and up until Cade, hadn't had a date or sex in equally as long. The more time the case took, the more I threw myself into it, convincing myself I must have missed something, and I was repeatedly going over the same information, desperate for a new clue.

But there was nothing, and after three years, I was being forced to face the fact that perhaps I was wasting my life. How could I let Dad down, though? It was so *wrong*, and it stung a sharp pain in my heart even to think of having to really let the case go and, therefore, letting Dad go.

What would I do without the case to focus on?

Live. Work. Be a cop. See friends.

Be with Cade.

It felt selfish.

My cell vibrated in my hand, making me jump and rousing me from my musings. Private number. I frowned as I stared at the screen. I didn't usually answer private numbers, but something about the continued ringing, long after a telemarketer would have given up, felt insistent.

Swiping to answer the call, I paused a beat before lifting the phone to my ear. "Hello?"

It wasn't quite silence on the other end. There was an unsettling static interference and breathing, steady and deep.

I wanted to hang up, but something made me ask again. "Hello?"

"Hello, Nikola."

The voice sent chills down my spine, and my

hand began to sweat around my cell. "Who is this?"

"A little birdy told me you've been investigating where you shouldn't."

My stomach lurched. Was I speaking to my father's murderer? My mouth was too dry to speak.

"This little birdy also told me…" he continued, adding ominous pauses that I couldn't be sure if they were for dramatic effect or not. Either way, it increased my nerves every time I had to listen to that static. "Apparently, you're quite relentless."

I found my voice again. "Who. Is. This?"

"I'm the sort of man you don't want the attention of, sweet Nikola."

"You killed him, didn't you?"

The responding chuckle was low and quiet, and I had to press the phone to my ear to hear his next words. "There comes a time in life when you must let things go, sweet girl. All your searching and questioning, all the work you do out of hours, you need to let it all go. I know it can't be easy. I'm a sentimental man myself, and right now, I'm doing some cleaning up and letting go of my own, and Nikola…" He paused, and I held my breath. "Don't let yourself become part of my cleanup, like my unfortunate little birdy, who talked an awful lot."

"*Who is this?*" I shouted into the phone, but he'd already hung up.

Dropping the phone onto the mattress, I sunk my face into my hands and groaned, allowing a moment for the trembling of my shoulders to subside. Whoever this man was, if he thought a phone call was going to dissuade me, he didn't know me at all. I didn't think I was close with my investigation, but apparently, I was upsetting someone by simply looking, so maybe I was closer than I thought.

Dad, what were you involved in?

Don't let yourself become part of my cleanup.

Is that what happened to Officer Kim? Was whoever this was jumping ship and tying up any loose ends before they did? And who was the *little birdy*?

Since I had to go to the station to hand in my handcuffs, it was the perfect opportunity to snoop around a bit and see if anything had happened that may have triggered the phone call.

How did he get my number?

But even more disturbing was the next question—*how much did he know about me?*

He knew who my father was, that I was investigating, and my name, that much I could verify. Did he know where I lived and worked? Was I being followed?

Casting a glance over my shoulder, I bound out of bed and yanked down the window blind in my bedroom. Suddenly, my home felt incredibly exposed. Despite the fact that there was no window access—someone would need to either break into my tiny courtyard and walk down the side of the house or scale a six-foot mesh fence to the bin area—every window felt like a threat now. I wanted desperately to go to the practice range and fire off a few shots, something to ease my mind and remind me I knew how to look after myself. But since I had to hand in my gun, I'd have to make do with the gym. Maybe someone there would be willing to spar with me.

I thought of Cade. *I like to fight,* he'd said.

Well, if he didn't already think I was a weirdo for asking him to a graveyard to mourn the loss of my father and then back to my place to search for misplaced handcuffs we'd use in an inappropriate sex game, he *certainly* would think I was strange if I asked him to *fight me* to work out some stress.

He might ask why I was so additionally stressed, and I didn't want him to worry. Cade seemed the type who would try to solve my problems for me, and a mystery man threatening my life wasn't something I wanted him involved in.

I was a cop.

I could handle this myself.

Because I'd done so well so far.

Sighing, I eyed my uniform, squeezing my eyes shut before settling on some jeans and a loose T-shirt. I'd have a shower when I got back, and maybe the running warm water would help me think because it was certainly too much to hope it could help me relax.

The drive to the station was quick and uneventful. I'd missed rush hour, and was in the small window before the lunch rush began. Striding into the station, I tried to keep my head high, feigning that the stares didn't bother me as I made my way to the front desk before sliding my handcuffs across the counter.

Lieutenant Niles was leaning on the edge of the counter, and I was about to offer a sheepish hello when I took a better look at his face. His brow was furrowed deeply, his lips pressed into a thin line, and one hand was halfway through combing his gray hair, gripping it lightly. I scribbled my signature on the required paperwork to complete the sign-over and walked over to him, tapping lightly on the counter with a fingernail next to his hand to gain his attention.

"Kline." He looked up, but his eyes weren't focused on me. "What are you doing here?"

"Handing in my cuffs."

"Right, right." He still wasn't really paying attention to me.

"What's wrong?"

Niles folded the piece of paper he'd been reading and finally met my eyes. "Nothing you need to worry about."

"Niles?"

He took a moment to stare at me, steel-gray eyes that penetrated mine, the same stare he'd given me in training when I had ruffled his feathers. I doubted he'd be exactly thrilled about my suspension, but there was an edge to his stare that pricked the hairs on the back of my neck, and I resisted the urge to rub my hand over them.

"How well did you know Karolina Torres?"

My back stiffened, and I glanced at the front door. I didn't want to be having this conversation, I had more important things to worry about. "We'd passed each other in the precinct, but I never worked with her. We had some... disagreements." Something clicked in my mind, and I eyed him suspiciously before realization dawned. "Wait, what do you mean *did* I know her?"

Niles threw a glance over my head at the officer at the counter. "Torres killed herself early this morning."

My throat constricted, and I fought the urge to cough or, even better, bend over and dry heave. This was too much.

No coincidences.

"What happened?" I asked.

"I know what you're thinking, and no, just no, Kline. Unlike Kim, she left a note."

I eyed the paper in his hand, which crumpled under his grip, his hand covered in a latex glove. Why would he use a glove to handle a suicide note? Unless... "You suspect something, don't you, sir?"

"Kline—"

"Was her bank account drained?" He didn't answer, but looking at his face, he didn't need to. "Let me see the note."

"No."

"Don't make me snatch it from you and get my fingerprints on it, Lute, I'm in enough trouble as it is." *Lute* instead of *Lieutenant*, I didn't use the abbreviation often, and never in front of others lest he be accused of some sort of favoritism simply because no one else had the balls to give him a nickname. But his eyes softened when he looked at me before darting around again.

"Fine, but don't fucking touch it."

He flicked it open, and I had to grip my T-shirt to stop myself from snatching it from him, practically inhaling it as I tried to get closer. I didn't know what Karolina's handwriting looked like, I'd only ever seen her signature. Was this normal for her? This messy scrawl, dotted with what I can only assume were tears.

This felt all wrong, dread already creeping down my back as I read the note.

> *I'm sorry.*
> *Mom, I love you. Please forgive me.*
> *I should have seen Kim's state of mind. I*
> *should have been able to save him.*
> *I've done nothing worthwhile, and my life*
> *will be reduced to evidence in a box. Don't*

*even open the box. Just leave it, and me be,
to die in piece.
Goodbye.*

Niles snatched it away, sliding it into an evidence bag before pulling off the gloves. He wasn't looking at me, and thoughts were swirling wildly through my mind.

Evidence in a box.

No coincidences.

Karolina and I had only yesterday fought in the evidence locker immediately *after* she checked out a box, then she had made some crack about my father.

Don't even open the box.

It was a warning, and if that wasn't obvious enough.

To die in piece.

No way she'd make that mistake, *piece* instead of *peace*?

It was a warning.

I swallowed. "How did she die?"

"Cut her wrists in the bath."

"Lute, please. There are clues in that note. She was warning me, and why would she warn me unless I was looking into something I shouldn't? Which means I was right, my father, Officer Kim, and now Torres—"

"Nikki." I stared at him. He hadn't used my first

name since... ever. His face was drained of color, and he whispered, "You need to let this all go. Just get on with your life."

My eyes searched his, and the pain I found there killed me. Niles turned away, telling me to go, relax a bit on my weeks off, try to reset, and get back to a good place. All those stock standard things you tell people when they have time off work, forced or otherwise.

"Lute... Niles," I pleaded with him. "Please. Please just *consider*—"

"I can't."

"Niles?"

"You don't understand, Nikki. Please, you need to let it go."

I watched as he walked away, but he didn't look back, and eventually, I had to leave the station before I caught the unwanted attention of Burke.

There were dirty cops. This wasn't news to me. *But Niles?* Surely not.

The pain in his eyes told me he knew what I wanted so desperately to know, but he either wouldn't or couldn't tell me.

Who the hell was I dealing with here?

CHAPTER
12

CADE

Frank wasn't kidding when he said his contact didn't blend in with humanity as we did. He was something out of a horror movie, and there was no way in Hell or Earth that humans would trust him or let him get close enough to gain any trust. Tall and lanky, his arms and legs appeared too long for his body. He dragged his fingers lazily over the dining table as I sat, and even the sound of his skin on the cheap pine was unnerving. His face rested in his other palm, not bored, simply observing me, and while I was comfortable in my strength, there was a dark power behind him that made my demon shift uncomfortably under my skin. Whether to get the fuck out of this house or to attack, I wasn't sure yet.

Attacking would be a mistake. His deep eyes watched me, withdrawn as though he was watching me from another world, another plane of existence. Short, shaved hair, thinning before he took a razor to it, sat atop a drawn-out face, ending in a harsh chin he tapped with his fingers as he finally leaned back in his chair, done with his study of me for now.

"Earl," I said simply as I settled back into my chair, the metal legs scraping noisily across the dirty linoleum. Earl lived in a cheap apartment, worse than mine, and cockroaches had scattered when he'd turned on the light. Something told me he didn't mind the insects.

"Frank sent you."

It wasn't a question, but I nodded anyway, and Earl's lips curled into a smile that only served to increase the sense of uneasiness that floated between us. I wasn't meant to tell him, but he already knew, and there'd be no sense in denying it.

"I need some information." There seemed little point bothering with small talk, and Earl simply raised an eyebrow lazily at me, returning his fingers to the dining table between us to resume his ministrations, tracing small circles and figure eights.

"Frank doesn't pay me enough to be giving out information." He glanced around the small room, there was barely space for his legs under the small two-person table, and I pushed my chair back, unwilling to make physical contact with him. Scowling, I shoved my hand in my pocket before rolling the small wad of cash across the table, another gift from Frank.

Earl smiled again, a lopsided grin that displayed the teeth on his left side more than his right. His long fingers curled around the cash, and he slid it from the table and into his pocket without counting it. "What do you want to know?"

"Three years ago, a man named Mitch Murphy was murdered. He was also known as Garrett Porter." Earl's eyebrows raised slightly, but he said nothing to interrupt, so I continued, "I want to know who killed him."

"Why?"

"*Why* I want to know is none of your fucking business."

He was neither offended nor concerned at my language and disrespectful tone, but there was a pulse of power that surged from him. I refused to flinch, but it made my stomach drop. He was the worst of the worst, exactly the sort of being you avoided even in Hell. A demon who, after centuries, had grown bored with torture and came to Earth to terrify the living. While I can't claim I was on Earth for anything noble, it was certainly a purer motivation than the demon who sat across from me now. Every second in this apartment was torture, and I wanted to get the hell out of there.

But I needed something first, anything to help Nikki.

Earl sighed, watching me, rolling his tongue around in his mouth as he thought. He knew something, it was written all over his face, but he was deciding how much to tell me, what information was worth three thousand dollars.

"There's a nightclub."

He stopped talking, and I grew impatient. Surely, that's not all he had to say. "And?"

"Murphy ran his business from there. He's dead, but the business is still going. You see?"

"The new owner killed him?"

Earl smirked. "I'm not saying that. I'm telling you only the facts."

"Which nightclub?"

He stared at me for a beat longer. "Urban."

I'd never heard of it, and I wondered if Nikki had. Surely, if it were the basis for her father's business, it would have come up in her research? But at the same time, she thought him to be a professional man, an upright citizen, and someone who dealt only in real estate wouldn't work out of a nightclub. Perhaps she didn't know. Someone in his position would have had the means and the knowledge to hide ownership of places he didn't want discovered, which led to the issues Nikki was having tracking down any information. The new owner, whoever he was, would have continued that web of paperwork, tangling it further until it was unbreakable. If you knew someone who knew someone, you would know where to go to source drugs or whatever it was you wanted. But Nikki? She had cop written all over her, and she was simply not the sort of person to give out huge bribes to those she had morality issues with only for information that may not pan out.

Not to mention she'd been searching under the wrong damn name.

"Is that all you have for me?" I asked, standing and moving around the back of my chair, gripping and holding it between us, ready to lift and brandish it like a lion tamer if he tried to reach for me with those intimidatingly long arms.

Earl watched me, his eyes rolling up before he gazed around the room lazily.

He moved to stand, and I grasped the chair.

There weren't many beings on Earth I had to look up to, but Earl's head almost scraped the low ceiling, the fluorescent lighting flickering obscenely behind him, creating a halo of sickly light around his head. He continued drumming his fingers on the table as he stood, and when he reached full height, his fingertips were only barely above the surface. Arms too long for his body, ready to sweep out and capture prey.

"One day..." he drawled and held my eye contact, "... I'll be making enough on my own that I won't need Frank's payoffs." Earl eyed me, his gaze increasing in intensity, and whatever whisper of a grin he had previously faded. "You'd be best to remind him of that. He's a means to an end but has no power over me."

"I'm not your messenger."

"You'll be wise to do what I ask of you, *puer*."

My back stiffened as my demon crawled under my skin, and I lifted my lip in a sneer before turning to leave, grinding my teeth and hoping he didn't follow me. Because I'm certain if his presence were behind me, I wouldn't be able to stop myself from attacking him.

Self-preservation tended to override logic with evil stalking at your back.

Smithy had a job for me, and the further I moved away from Earl's, the more my mind cleared and allowed me to think. I had information, a single piece of information that could assist Nikki. The question now was, how to get it to her without her knowing it had come from me? Would she believe an anonymous tip? She'd spent years poking around and asking questions and had almost certainly made herself known with all the wrong people. It wasn't completely out of the realm of reality that someone would have a guilty conscience and step forward to offer their assistance in the form of information.

Like me and my guilty conscience.

When this was over and Nikki had her answers, what was I expecting? Could I hide my nature from her forever? Was *forever* even something I was considering with a human? I wanted her in a way beyond the physical, although fucking her every day piqued something in me. She was mine, a possessive demonic nature that I couldn't crush, as I acknowledged I could never be human.

Not that I wanted to be, but now there was part of me that wanted Nikki without the complication of my true nature and all this other bullshit that came with it.

There was no one I could talk to. Frank would scoff and tell me to simply fuck her and move on. I thought of talking to Smithy—he certainly seemed the type to confide in. In my mind's eye, I imagined him chuckling at my debacle, worrying over a woman. He'd scratch his slight beer gut through his work shirt and tell me I'd be better to ask his wife, Maria.

I bet when they were courting thirty-two years ago, they never had to worry about the things I did.

Hey, babe, I tortured your father, and now I may hold the secret to his death.

Fuck. This situation was too much.

If I wasn't at home in Hell, and I wasn't cut out to face issues on Earth, what did that make me? Less of a man, certainly no demon. I was a being without a home when all I wanted to do was set up and play house, and then every night drive my cock into Nikki's pussy, falling asleep only when she was so exhausted she couldn't move.

It sounded like heaven to me, though I had no point of comparison.

My skin started to crawl as I neared the corner of Smithy's shop, and I growled. Without even knowing what, all I knew was *something* was wrong. My heart rate began to increase, a drum rhythm against the inside of my chest as I picked up the pace. My veins widened, and I had to take a few steadying breaths to keep my demon from coming to the surface.

Whatever the danger was, my senses were picking up on it. If I couldn't handle it in my human form, only then would I let the demon out.

I found Smithy backed against the front counter, his fingers gripping the dented and paint-stained wood as a young woman was invading his space. Snarling when I entered the shop, she turned to face me, her eyes flashing with malice and teeth bared.

Like recognizes like.

Demon.

"What the fuck is going on?" There was no point in hiding the aggression in my tone. This wasn't a friendly visit, and the sweat on Smithy's head was evident in the bright lighting of the shop, his eyes wide and darting between us.

The young demon turned and flicked her long black hair over her shoulder as she faced me. "Nothing, nothing at all." Keeping her in my peripheral vision, I watched Smithy as she left the shop. He said nothing but didn't visibly relax until she was out the door.

I frowned, and Smithy opened his mouth to protest.

Launching after her, I caught up with her a few shops down, and she hissed at me as I grabbed her throat and held her against the warm bricks of the nearest building, her toes barely scraping the ground. "What the fuck do you want? Who are you?"

Her eyes flashed yellow, and I increased my grip on her neck. She was young, remarkably young, and if this came down to a matter of physical strength, she'd lose. I'm certain she could feel that, her pulse beating a rapid tune against my hand, slowly calming as she took a moment to compose herself. "I'm no one. I'm simply doing a job."

"What job?" I growled out and shook her slightly when she went to open her mouth. *"Don't lie to me."*

"Smith was late on his protection payment. I was simply there to remind him."

"What protection payment?"

She rolled her eyes, and they widened at the top

of the arch when I increased my grip again, easing it only to let her response out. "Surely, you know who runs this city? If local businesses don't want trouble, they pay the fees and look the other way."

"What about the police?"

She barked out a harsh laugh. "Half of them are in on it."

Not my Nikki, though. These are the very people she's fighting against.

"Who sent you?"

She snarled at me. "I'll tell you this, fuckboy, I may not be particularly loyal, but I'm more scared of him than I am of *you.*"

"I can kill you."

"You can't... there are rules." She was right, and I snarled. Demons can't kill on Earth, human or otherwise. We'd end up back in Hell if we were allowed to live at all.

"And your boss isn't governed by those same rules?" I spat out.

Her expression changed, going blank, and she paused before answering, "No."

What the fuck?

I tried a different tack. "When you came to Earth, how did you know where to go to find work?"

"Everyone knows if you want cash for violence, you go to the club."

"What club?"

"Urban." She rolled her eyes again.

Urban. Nikki doesn't believe in coincidences, and therefore, neither would I. "Who runs it?"

"How about you go and find out for yourself? I'm no snitch."

"How come I've never heard of it?"

She bit her bottom lip. It wasn't a pensive look but cruelty in those eyes, the look of a demon who knew little but thought she knew it all. "If you hadn't heard, then nobody back home told you..." she paused, then laughed, the sound biting into me, "... and if nobody thought you should know, then you're no demon."

Growling, I shoved her hard against the wall, and while she grunted and winced, there was little satisfaction in the act. Because she was right. I never fit in, and if there was a place demons came to while on Earth for some quick cash to run errands of a violent nature, I wouldn't have been told.

Who the hell was running that club?

Someone not governed by the rules that demons were bound by—no killing of humans. Yet someone who knew not only the existence of demons but used them for their strength and lust for violence for their own gain. A human? It seemed unlikely.

If a demon was responsible for the death of Nikki's father, then I was in deeper than I thought.

"Are you going to let me go?"

In response, I tightened my grip on her throat,

cutting off her air supply as I pushed my palm painfully into the soft part of her neck. I could feel her throat working against my hand, and her mouth opened as her body became desperate for the air it was being denied. But her eyes were calm because she had the upper hand. Not only could I not kill her, but she knew she had gotten me with the quip about me not being in the loop for the work on Earth. I didn't frighten nor intimidate her.

But apparently, whoever ran Urban, did.

Letting her go, she dropped to her feet, rubbing her neck and glaring at me. The rage was still bubbling in my veins, and my demon was close to the surface. If she wanted to fight, to engage me in this state, then I was all for it. There was no gender bias amongst demons, male versus female violence wasn't uncommon, and it certainly wasn't always the male who came out on top.

I could take her, and I welcomed the challenge that sat on the tip of her tongue.

She shrugged and flicked her hair over her shoulder again before striding away.

Gaining new information had done nothing to ease my guilt. It had only made it worse because now I had some information that could potentially break open Nikki's case, but it was fraught with danger I didn't yet know the nature of. Going behind her back tugged at that damn reminder in my chest that I actually fucking cared about someone, and the burden only twisted the knife further, making my lip lift into a scowl as I shoved my hands in my pockets and moved to see if Smithy was okay.

Looks like it was time for me to leave a clue for Nikki about Urban.

But when she went to investigate, I'd be there to protect her.

CHAPTER 13

NIKKI

Giddy like a schoolgirl, I leaned against my front door frame, watching Cade make his way up the short cobble-stoned pathway, the stones darkened and slick with moisture from the light afternoon shower. He had stepped out of a large white moving truck parked outside my place, a rare free spot. Cade's smile flicked on and off, a similar reaction happening to the frown that came and went from his brow. My grin dropped as I watched him. It was near impossible to tell what he was thinking, but Cade had become my escape from reality, as well as much more than that, and I half expected him to jump me and fuck me on the floor the second he arrived. But something was on his mind.

As he passed my mailbox, he gestured vaguely at it, and I shrugged. "Haven't checked it in a few days." Without a word, Cade nodded and opened the rusted white dome top, pulling out a small handful of envelopes and handing them to me as he reached the porch. "Hi," I said.

"Hi, angel." His eyes were on mine, and I tilted my chin up expectantly. With a smirk, Cade traced his thumb along my jawline before pressing a kiss to my lips, sweeping his tongue across mine and humming. "I'm going to taste your sweet cunt tonight," he whispered against my lips, and I shuddered, barely managing to stumble inside and close the door behind us.

Flicking through the mail, I stopped in the hall before it opened to the living room. Cade turned around a moment later. "What's up?"

Frowning, I dropped the letters onto the floor, stepping over them and rummaging through a drawer to pull out some gloves before picking them up again. Discarding the junk mail and a bill I'd like to hope I'd already paid, my fingers trembled as I ran them over the edge of the final envelope.

Cade came up to my side and slid an arm around my waist. I leaned into him, but when he went to touch the letter in my hands, I yanked it from him, crying out, "Don't touch it!"

"Why?"

"Fingerprints."

Was this from *him?* The man who had threatened me earlier? My name was simply printed on the front with a thick black pen that had run slightly with the droplets of rain. No logo, no return address, not even a stamp. The letter had been hand-delivered.

Had he been here?

Trembling, I tore the letter open carefully and read it. One line only.

If you're looking for whoever killed your father, go to Urban.

Cade read over my shoulder, his back tensing as I stared intently at the paper in my hands. Pulling away from him, I found a resealable plastic bag and dropped the letter and the envelope inside, adding it to one of the new piles of paperwork we had made near the fireplace.

"Urban," I said.

Cade nodded. "I saw."

The adrenaline was surging through me. Where had the note come from? And why now? With the recent deaths of Kim and Torres, maybe someone was getting cold feet. Maybe the mystery man's endeavor to clean up all his loose ends had resulted in some guilty consciences coming to the surface. Even if they were simply hoping I'd catch him before he got to them, it was the first new clue I'd had in years.

Urban, why didn't that sound familiar? I knew

there were buildings in my father's name I didn't know of, and while he owned several clubs, I'm certain Urban wasn't one of them. Not one of the ones I could trace anyway. The properties I had been able to track from him had all disappeared under networks of name changes and paperwork. I'd even checked under my brother's and mother's names, and Urban didn't appear anywhere.

Still, the note didn't say it was one of his buildings but simply indicated that whoever was there might know something. I'd need to find the new owner, no sense in wasting my time with staff anymore. I had to go straight to the source.

A new energy was pulsing through me just when I was on the verge of giving myself a break before it destroyed me entirely. While I tried to calm myself to let the logical part of my brain remind me that this could be nothing but another dead end, I needed to believe it was more than that.

"I'm going," I said, grabbing a jacket from the nearest pile.

"Now?" Cade's eyes widened, and I threw him an impatient look. *What difference did it make?*

"The club is more likely to be occupied at night."

Cade was clenching and releasing his fists, and I stared at him for a moment before grabbing my keys and phone and shoving them in my jacket pockets. For a moment, I contemplated taking a weapon but thought the better of it. Chances are I'd be patted down before even stepping foot in the club.

"Are you coming or not?"

Cade's lip lifted into what was almost a snarl, and my eyebrows involuntarily shot up. "Of course, I'm coming."

"Good." I strode toward the front door, grabbing his hand on the way. "You can drive."

Cade's hand gripped mine, and with strength I'd only seen hints of, he tugged me back toward him, spinning me until I collided with his chest with a grunt. As I went to squirm away, he grabbed my shoulders and waited until I looked into his blazing eyes. "If anything happens, you get behind me, okay?"

"I don't need you to protect me. I'm a cop, remember?"

Running a hand through his hair, he huffed out his impatience. "I know, but I'm stronger than you."

"Why? Because you're the *man?*"

He snarled again. "Because I'm..." His jaw clenched as he grit his teeth. "Because I care, okay?"

Narrowing my gaze, I watched his face before rolling my eyes and saying, "Fine." I was too full of energy to argue with him. I wanted to be at Urban already and find out what secrets this club held.

Finally, a clue.

I guess Cade was my good luck charm.

The music assaulted my eardrums the second the door was opened, and Cade stayed so close behind me I could feel the brush of his jacket against my back. His fingers remained splayed protectively on my waist, and I smiled at the sensation. I hadn't been romantically involved with such a protective man before, tending to avoid them because I didn't want to deal with the excess testosterone. But there was something soothing about Cade's presence. Beyond his physical stature, which was impressive in itself, he simply radiated a quiet power, and the crowd parted as we made our way through to the bar.

Cade waved two fingers at the bartender, who approached and leaned forward to hear us over the music. "We need to see the boss."

"I'm the manager here," she answered, tucking her curls behind an ear and frowning.

Cade leaned forward to meet her halfway across the bar, and her instinct to move away from him made me smirk. "The *boss.* You know *exactly* who I mean."

Her eyes widened, and her gaze darted back and forth between Cade's pupils before she scurried off.

"Now we wait," I said.

Cade nodded, leaning against the bar. But for once, his stance was anything but relaxed, his back and shoulders tense. He moved to pull me against him, and when I resisted, he growled, grabbing my waist and yanking me back until my ass nestled against his crotch. Normally, I'd take advantage of the position, but Cade being on such high alert was sending my senses into overdrive. Did he know something about this place I didn't? I kept my gaze moving, never settling on one person or spot for too long, taking a mental inventory of the occupants.

Wait.

When I tensed, Cade followed my gaze, and seeing nothing in particular, he stared at me. "What is it?"

I frowned. I could have sworn I saw my brother, but what would he be doing here? This didn't seem like his scene. When I hadn't seen him in so long, I'd assumed he'd left the city. I searched again for him but saw no one I recognized. Cade asked me again what I was looking at.

"Nothing," I lied.

An attractive woman with black hair approached us, and another growl rumbled through Cade's chest as he pulled me closer to him. "You!" Cade snarled.

She cocked a perfectly plucked eyebrow at him, her eyes appearing cat-like with the eyeliner around them. "I don't think we've met." She let her gaze slide to me, her lip lifting into a smirk as she took in my hair—I wasn't in the mood to be called *innocent* or some shit, not tonight—before she returned her eyes to Cade. "Follow me."

Once again, I was yanked backward as I moved to follow. Cade kept me behind him as we weaved our way through the crowd. Okay, the overprotectiveness was starting to get on my nerves now, and Cade cried out as I twisted his arm behind his back before ducking under his elbow, being the first to follow the woman with black hair up a narrow staircase. She turned at the sound and smirked at the rage on Cade's face and my impassive expression before continuing up the winding staircase.

At the top, she tapped on the door a few times, the music was muted slightly, and the purple lighting cast eerie shadows around the stairs. When the door swung open, the staircase was flooded with both light and sound as we stepped out onto a balcony overlooking the club.

"Visitors for you, Emrick, sir," she said.

The décor screamed of someone who had money and wanted everyone to know it, and sitting upon the velvety chair opposite us, a man with sunglasses and a hoodie pulled over his head had his fingers together in a pyramid, resting his chin on his fingertips.

Wishing I could see his eyes beyond the dark sunglasses, I simply stared at him. Up until this moment, adrenaline had surged me forward, but once that door to the staircase behind us was closed with a definitive click, my skin started to crawl. It was him, the man in the chair, he radiated darkness and danger, and I rolled my shoulders, trying to rid myself of the feeling which settled over us.

The dark-haired woman had disappeared back down the stairs, and we were left with the man in the chair, who I assumed to be the boss, and a handful of his bodyguards who stood at strategic spots around the balcony, no corner left unprotected.

"Who are you?" he barked. He didn't need much volume to his voice, and I got the sense he could silence a room with a wave of his hand. Nerves overtook me, and I dug my nails into my palms to stop myself from trembling. Casting a quick glance at Cade, I did a double-take when I saw his expression.

Fear.

Cade's jaw was tensing and twitching, a nervous tick I hadn't seen from him before. I wasn't the only one making fists at my sides, but Cade's muscles also flexed on his neck. He was preparing for a fight.

Did he know this Emrick?

"I'm here for information," I said, surprising myself at how steady I managed to keep my voice.

Why was I so afraid? I don't even know what I was expecting, but it wasn't this man who made my skin crawl, and I suppressed a shudder at the idea of him coming closer to me.

Please stay in your chair.

Turning his head slowly, he was now looking at me, and although I couldn't see his eyes, I could certainly feel the power of his gaze drilling into me.

"Who. Are. You?" he repeated.

"My name is Nikki, and I've been investigating my father's murder."

"I don't know him."

My eyebrows raised. "You might. Garrett Porter."

The slightest twitch of Emrick's dark eyebrow betrayed him, and he lowered his hands to his lap, drumming his fingers against his knee while he continued to stare at me. There was a movement of his cheeks like he was running his tongue along his teeth or rolling it in his mouth, maybe trying to decide what to say or do.

"What makes you think I know anything about it?" he finally asked.

"Anonymous tip."

Somehow his laugh was worse than his gritted-teeth frustration, and he barked out a single note of amusement. Still chuckling, Emrick slid off his sunglasses, and I took a step back from him.

Black, his eyes were black. The irises were so dark they were barely indistinguishable from the pupil. I'd never seen anything like it, and there was something so distinctly unnatural about it. I'd have sworn he was wearing contacts, but he hardly seemed the type to bother.

No wonder he wore the damn sunglasses, he was terrifying.

Standing, Emrick made his way across the floor in a handful of strides, but he stopped in front of Cade, ignoring me almost entirely. They were similar heights, and while Cade was no lightweight, Emrick's arms were huge, like he spent every spare second working out, and it simply added to the intimidation factor. To Cade's credit, he didn't flinch but held Emrick's eye contact while they stared each other down.

"And where do you come into this?" Emrick asked.

Cade sneered at him. "None of your business."

"Aww," Emrick cooed, and I wanted to take Cade's hand, more for my comfort than for his. "I think it is my business." He turned his gaze to me, and I was hypnotized by the darkness of his eyes. Beyond the color, or lack of it, there was real darkness there. I'd dealt with many criminals since being a cop, and I'd never felt this way in the presence of another human being before.

The thought hit me like a bolt of lightning—*if this man tried to pay me off to keep my mouth shut, I might consider it just to get him to leave me alone.*

Suddenly, I felt bad for Niles.

Fuck. We were in deep.

"What did your father do for a living?" Emrick asked me.

"He worked in real estate."

Another laugh from Emrick, and I frowned. "Really? Are you sure about that?"

"I…" I'd had no reason *not* to be sure. Why would Dad lie to me? But the creeping feeling up my spine told me that Emrick knew something I didn't, something I wasn't sure I wanted to know. The urge to run made my feet tingle. I'd never been one to run from my problems, but this room and all the people in it, aside from Cade, made me feel ill.

"Tell you what, Nikki. If your boyfriend here tells you what he knows about your father, I'll tell you what I know."

I turned to Cade, still staring at Emrick, his jaw tense and visibly shaking with rage. Emrick was smirking, almost daring Cade with his eyes to initiate a fight. "Cade, what's he talking about? You don't know anything. We just met."

When Cade didn't speak, Emrick moved to stand closer to him, invading his space as much as possible without touching him, toe-to-toe and chest-to-chest, neither man moving as they stared hard at each other. "Oh, I think he knows a lot more than he's telling you, sweet thing."

"Shut up," Cade snapped.

Emrick simply grinned.

"Cade?" I whispered.

"You better tell her, or I will," Emrick snarled out.

Reaching up to touch Cade's arm, he tensed under his jacket at my touch, but I didn't pull away. "Cade, what's going on?"

Emrick had moved away to sit back down, crossing his ankle over his knee and leaning back, watching us as though we were his personal entertainment. Cade looked at the floor, grinding his teeth as a flush worked its way up his neck.

"Your father wasn't who you think he was, Nikki," he said after a pause. Sighing, he raised his eyes to mine, shining with pain and uncertainty.

"Turns out your boyfriend isn't who you think he is either." Emrick chuckled, and I ignored him. I wanted to know what Cade knew.

Swallowing against the dryness in my mouth and throat, I asked, "What do you mean?"

"Your father..." Cade closed his eyes before looking at me again. "His real name was Mitch Murphy. I assume he created the alias to protect his family." Cade tossed a look at Emrick, who smirked, and Cade snarled in return. "He ran a large underground crime network in this city, one of the most powerful. He wasn't a good man. He killed several people and made his money at the expense of the less fortunate using intimidation and torture. Beyond that, his fortune was grown from drugs and illegal gambling."

The sound from the club's music was muted, and the room was shrinking to engulf me, the walls moving in and the lights too bright. Swallowing again, I licked my lips. *God, I needed a drink.* But not water, something stronger. Why would he be telling me this? Why was Cade saying these things?

"You're lying," I choked out.

He shook his head, slow, remorseful movements. "I'm sorry, angel, but I'm not." He gestured around the club. "This was his. He ran his business from here."

"But..."

But *what?* What was I going to say?

Dad was an extraordinarily rich man, but you can become rich from working in real estate if you know what you're doing. And so what if he went away a lot on business trips? That wasn't unusual for someone in his position.

But all the properties? They simply disappeared when he was killed. Expertly.

So if his murder wasn't a crime organization taking my father out for his properties and assets, then it was...

"A change of ownership," I said quietly.

Turning to Emrick, he still had that smug fucking grin plastered on his face. My world falling around my shoulders was amusing to him, and he took pleasure in the fact that he had *caused* my pain.

What kind of sick fuck did that?

"You," I said, pointing at Emrick, "If this was my father's business, and it's yours now, then *you* killed him. You fucking monster!"

Cade's fingers scraped my arm as he reached out to grab me, but I launched myself across the room, desperate to get my hands around Emrick's neck, and was met with the solid wall which was the chest of one of his guards. He'd been on the other side of the room—his reflexes must have been incredible to get in front of me so quickly. I struggled against his hold, but he spun me and wrapped his arms around me, crushing my arms to my sides as I kicked out and fought against him. Cade cried out for him to let me go as he, too, was grabbed, but he didn't go down as easy. It took three of the men to restrain him, pressing him against the floor and using their weight to hold him down as he continued to writhe.

Emrick stood again, and when he traced a finger down my cheek, I shuddered. "Shh..." he shushed me gently, the sound crawling against my skin and sending goose bumps exploding across my arms. "Nikki, Nikki, Nikki... what a shock this must be for you." He continued to touch my cheek, and I snapped my teeth at him, hating the way he laughed as he drew his hand away from my face. "Look into my eyes, Nikki." Reluctantly I did and couldn't look away as he held my gaze, taking a long moment to simply stare at me before he stated resolutely, "I didn't kill your father."

We stared at each other for a beat longer.

I believed him.

"You could be making this up," I said, grasping at straws and hoping.

Emrick stalked off, disappearing into a door behind where he had sat. I remained in the hold of the bouncer until Emrick returned and shoved a framed picture in my hand. Craning my neck to look over the large arm of the man who held me, I took in the image of my father, feet up on a large desk, cigar in mouth, and stacks of cash on either side of him.

"This doesn't prove anything," I spat. "So he came to the club? So what?"

Emrick ignored me. "He was a vain fucker. Who keeps photos of themselves in their office anyway? But there are a dozen employees still here who would ID him as Mitch." Emrick's lip curled into a sneer, amusement flashing in his eyes. "And all of those would attest to the type of man he was, if you fancy to question them. But perhaps you're not ready to hear what a sick fuck he was. He was me before *I* was me."

"Do you know who killed him?" I asked again, but my certainty that I wanted to know the truth was ebbing away with each passing moment. Emrick claimed that people could identify my father as

Mitch Murphy, but they were under Emrick's employ and wouldn't tell me anything unless instructed.

But what did Emrick have to gain from lying to me?

This isn't where I thought this investigation would lead. When I saw the club, I assumed that it would lead me to the people responsible for Dad's murder, not an unwelcome revelation about his history. A revelation I wasn't convinced I was certain of.

But doubt was a powerful motivator.

"I don't know," Emrick said, brushing his fingers across my chin lightly and smirking when I yanked myself away from his touch. "And that's another truth. I will say that if I had known everything your father was responsible for before I took over, I'd have gladly killed him myself. But sometimes, information takes a while to come to light." He cast a look over my shoulder at Cade. "But the truth *always* comes out."

He turned away again, and the guard released me. I stood still, rubbing my arms. "You said you'd tell me what you knew," I demanded.

Emrick assessed me. "And I did, and what I know is nothing. I didn't kill Murphy. He was killed by one of the many enemies he made along the way. When I took over, he lost the protection of his business, and without it, he was taken down." His brow quirked. "I'm surprised his entire family wasn't killed."

"He protected us."

"So it seems." Emrick seemed unimpressed, as though my father protecting me meant nothing compared to what else he had done.

"Did you take his properties?" I demanded.

Emrick smirked again. "Of course. He signed them over to me, willingly, once he knew the alternative." When his eyes raked over my body, I shuddered again, imagining what threats he had promised against Dad and his family, against *me*.

"But you didn't kill him?"

Emrick lifted a shoulder. "There was no need." He sneered again, only serving to darken his expression. "Sometimes the stories that come out of survivors are more intimidating than a head on a stake, you see?"

Frowning, I stared at my feet. I didn't move. This was too much, and I needed time to think.

And Cade...

Turning, Cade was straightening after being released from the crushing hold of the guards. When he met my eyes, he shrunk away from my gaze. "Nikki, I'm sorry."

"You knew? You knew this whole time." My hands twitched, I didn't know if I wanted to slap him or throw my hands up in frustration. "Is this some sick joke to you? Did you know who I was when we met?"

"No, I swear I didn't. I only found out later—"

"Why didn't you tell me?"

"I didn't want to hurt you," Cade said, raising his voice.

Screwing my face up, I shook my head. "I need to go."

"Let me take you home."

"Stay the fuck away from me, Cade!"

The guard at the door didn't try to stop me and unlocked it, allowing me to run past and make my way down, the swirling of the winding staircase matching the chaos in my mind.

CHAPTER
14

CADE

As I shoved my way past the guard, I could hear Emrick laughing at my retreating back. That evil son of a bitch, he knew what I was the second I crossed the threshold, and it was only a matter of guesswork from there to figure out how I was involved with this situation. He took a stab in the dark and hit his target, twisting the knife to cause the most damage without having to lift a finger. The chances were slim I'd revealed my true nature to Nikki, and even less so that I had tortured her father in Hell.

Damn you, Emrick.

He was no angel.

His celestial power radiated from him, and although Nikki wouldn't have understood it, she responded in the same way she responded to my nature when we first met. But instead of arousal, it was fear prickling at her neck. She'd managed to keep herself mostly composed and in control until Emrick had driven a wedge between us and cut through my heart at the same time. The betrayal and pain in Nikki's eyes were almost enough to bring me to my knees. I never wanted to hurt her. I only wanted to help so she could move forward with her life.

Now her heart was broken, her world was shattered, and it was my fault.

Catching up with Nikki as she reached the bottom of the stairs, she shoved hard at my chest when I reached out to her. Our first night together, she had been interested in challenging me to a fight for fun, but now she was fighting in earnest, knocking my hands out of the way whenever I reached for her and snarling at me, angry tears prickling her eyes as I grabbed her arm.

"Get the fuck away from me," Nikki cried and attempted to pry my fingers from her arm. We were making a scene, and people in the club started noticing. However, we'd descended the stairs, and it seemed that whatever went on up there, people knew to look the other way, quickly turning away after glancing at us.

"I know you hate me, but I'm not letting you go home by yourself."

She continued to fight, and I grunted when she

landed a punch against my abs. Nikki hissed through her teeth, shaking her fist out as the hit would have hurt her more than it did me. I didn't want to fight her, not like this, but she was becoming increasingly agitated, and her attacks grew wilder until I was forced to pick her up and throw her over my shoulder.

The bouncers cast a disinterested glance as I moved through the club, Nikki continuing to punch at my back and kicking against my stomach, yelling at me to put her down. My jaw ached from how hard I ground my teeth together, the guilt and injustice of the situation stirring up the bile in my stomach and twisting my gut into knots.

Nikki didn't stop fighting even as we broke out onto the street, the cool air assaulting my senses after the sweat and heat of the club. She wouldn't still and screamed with rage when I shoved her into the back of the truck before I slammed the large doors shut and locked them. The drive back to her place was accompanied by the relentless pounding of her fists against the inside of the truck, screaming obscenities at me. There was no point in saying anything, and nothing I could say would douse the flames of hatred she had for me now.

This wasn't what I wanted to happen.

Anger continued to bubble inside me, and my demon stirred.

I hadn't given in to my need for sex or violence

recently, and with all the emotions stirring inside me, I was on the edge of losing control.

Pulling onto Nikki's street, the symphony of crashing and screaming from the back of the truck had subsided, and when I dropped out of the cabin, my boots sounding heavy against the road, and opened the back, Nikki was curled up in the far corner. Her knees were pulled up to her chest, her face was flushed red with her hair hanging around her shoulders, and her cheeks a sweaty mess.

But there was no more anger.

She was crying now.

Inside my chest, my heart simply broke.

I never believed it possible.

Everyone's heard the figure of speech—your heart breaking—but I didn't expect it to feel like this. It was like a cavern opened up behind my ribs, leaving a black hole that widened further as I reached my hand into the truck, and she cowered from me.

"Nikki, please," I choked out, my voice hitching before I grit my teeth again. "I just wanted to bring you home."

I expected questions from her, a barrage of screaming and accusations. But the way she stood and brushed the sawdust from the truck off her pants and jacket before striding past me, ignoring my outstretched hand and jumping gracefully from the truck, cut deep. Her lips were pressed together in a thin line, and she stared at me, a thousand things left unsaid running between us while the world of emotions played across her hazel eyes.

Without a word, she spun on her heel and stormed to her house, locking the door behind her with a definitive click.

I didn't follow.

There's a social norm for how to deal with many situations—how long you should wait before calling after a first date or sex, how to correctly respond to *how are you* when asked by a cashier at a shop, how long you shake hands with a stranger before letting go.

But how long should you wait before contacting someone who's just found out her father was a criminal, information which was revealed by the man she had been dating and trusted, who then kidnapped and threw her in the back of a truck? There was no social protocol for that.

I could only manage one night before I went back to her. While there wasn't anything I could say to make things right, I simply couldn't stay away. With an ache in my chest, I was drawn to Nikki, an ache I knew could only be solved by holding her against me and hoping she could forgive me as I tried desperately to shove away the reminder she didn't even know the worse of it yet.

Would it have been better to reveal the full truth? I could feel Emrick's eyes on me last night as I left out the information about what I was and how I knew Murphy, but he said nothing, instead throwing in some cryptic crap about the truth always coming out. What was *his* truth? I wanted to know because then maybe I could use it against him as he had mine. Although something told me there wasn't much I could do or say to Emrick that would affect him at all, he was already surrounded by darkness.

Nikki wasn't home, and I leaned against the truck thinking while trying to put myself in her shoes. I'd explained to Smithy I was having *personal issues,* which somehow he knew meant it involved a woman, and he said as long as I completed my deliveries today, he was happy for me to use the truck to get where I needed to go to solve my problems.

At this point, I think I knew where I needed to be.

The truck rumbled along, the journey to the graveyard this time a stark contrast to my experience with Nikki's driving when we went together. Even if I put my foot on the accelerator and pushed it to the floor, it wouldn't reach the speeds her little car could on a bad day. This normally wouldn't bother me, but today I was grinding my teeth because every second I was away from her after I'd decided to find her was grating against my nerves.

And my demon was stirring.

Demons don't deal with emotions well. Hell, we rarely bother with them. But all this shit I was feeling was welling up inside me, and I had no idea how to cope with it. So my instincts told me to fight it out of my system or fuck it out.

I doubted Nikki would be in the mood to want sex with me right now.

Finally pulling into the graveyard parking lot, I sprinted across the field, ignoring the looks of indignation from the few mourners scattered around, and slowed only when the graveyard changed from the lush green grass to the broken garden beds and small stones.

Silence encased me once I stopped walking and the crunch of my boots subsided.

"No picnic this time?" I asked.

Nikki didn't turn around. She was kneeling at her father's grave, and I couldn't tell if she was looking at the headstone or the ground. Maybe she had her eyes closed in silent prayer, hoping she could reach him and get some answers.

"What are you doing here?"

She didn't move as I kneeled beside her, not even

when I swept a lock of her hair from her face and tucked it behind her ear. The usual pink of her cheeks was darker, her face blotchy from crying and anger. Betrayal would do that to a person, and I had to remind myself it wasn't only me who'd betrayed her. Her father had lied to her. Whether he did it to protect her or himself was irrelevant. She loved and trusted him far longer than she'd known me, and she'd be grappling with that as well.

I wanted it to be all about me, selfishly, and I wanted all of her attention, even if all that was directed at me was hatred.

"I came to say I'm sorry," I said.

"Okay."

She turned to me, leaning back on her heels and placing her hands on her knees, waiting.

"Um," I started, and she raised an eyebrow at me. "I'm sorry," I said lamely, watching her eyes for a clue as to what she wanted to hear from me, "I'm sorry I didn't tell you what I knew... I was only trying to protect you."

"Protect me from the truth, or were you just trying to protect yourself?"

"To protect *you*," I insisted, and she nodded as though she believed me but looked into the distance, her eyes unfocused. The wind brushed her hair along her cheek, and when she stared back at me, something in her eyes had changed.

"What do you think of me?" she asked.

There weren't a thousand things that swirled around in my mind at her question. In fact, there was only one. She was Nikki, a strong presence that had forced herself irrevocably into my mind and heart, but how do I explain that to her? I didn't think I could. Nor would this be the right time because her eyes weren't shimmering with tears, but swirling with emotion and rage, and I feared she hated me.

"Nikki—"

"I'm not some weak little girl, you know? I'm not scared and upset, sitting here clutching to the gravestone and crying *why God, why.*" She glanced at the gravestone, scoffing quietly. "I'm *pissed off,* Cade. Because if all this *is* true, then the man I loved most in the world *lied* to me for as long as I knew him. Then you come along, and you lie to me too, and I felt..." she trailed off.

What?

She felt *what?*

I wanted to know. Did she feel what I was feeling? These emotions can't have been as foreign to her as they were to me. Demons didn't *feel* things, and we certainly didn't admit it. Emotions were weakness, and my susceptibility to them had already made me an outcast at home.

How to tell her without actually telling her? I could only think of one thing. I wanted to tear her clothes off, claim her, and fuck her with everything

I had until she came undone. There wasn't an inch of her body I didn't want to touch because I knew already the way her nipples hardened under my fingers and tongue and the taste of her. I knew how she clenched around me as she came and the slight tremble of her leg as she came down from her high. There was nothing in this world as intoxicating as the feel of her, and nothing else would do.

Demons weren't known for being good with words. I could use my fuck-me voice all I wanted, but there was no meaning behind it. But there was one thing I did know, and it was the connection that existed when we came together, the air between and around us simply exploded with electricity.

I'd never get enough.

Nikki watched me, and I couldn't read her face. Her pupils shifted slightly as her gaze darted between my eyes, not focusing on either one. Then she bit her lip, my expression darkened, and there was a change in the air.

My back hit the ground as she launched at me, and I landed with the edging of the adjoining grave digging uncomfortably into my lower back, but I didn't care. Nikki's body was on top of mine, her breasts pressed against my chest, free from the restraints of a bra she hadn't bothered with, and I groaned at the feeling as she shoved her tongue in my mouth. She was so hot, the heat of her surrounding me as she ground her hips against the growing bulge in my pants.

This was wrong. *I shouldn't touch her. I should be talking to her and making this right,* I thought, even as I ran my hands down her back, grabbing her ass and pulling her against me as she moaned into my mouth.

Fuck.

A growl rumbled through my throat as my demon stirred. The scent of her arousal was in the air between us, and I wanted to taste her, to swallow her moans and her cum, and fuck her until she couldn't walk.

We were on top of her father's grave.

Fuck.

"Nikki—" My protest was cut off as she grabbed my face with both hands, silencing me with a passionate exchange of lips, tongues, and teeth, desperation seeping off her. She wanted release, needed to forget, and whether she was confused or angry or all of the above, she wanted *me.*

I couldn't deny her, not when her hands wandered down over my shoulders and arms, nails digging into my skin with a pain so sweet and pleasure I didn't deserve. There was nothing I wouldn't give her, and if what she wanted and needed was me, then she could have me, *all of me.*

No more questions, not now.

Rolling over, I flipped Nikki around so she was underneath me, and she let me take control, panting as I kissed my way down her body. I shoved her top up, bundling it so I could graze my teeth along the erect bud of her nipple and growling again as she moaned. I needed *more.* Yanking her boots and pants off, I discarded them, nestling myself between her legs and breathing in her scent. The small damp patch on the front of her underwear was all I needed to know, and I pressed my tongue over the fabric, rolling it over her lips and clit. Nikki grabbed at my hair, swearing and moaning, writhing under my touch.

She was mine, and I wasn't going to let her go, not now, not ever. Even if she never forgave me and I had to satiate myself by watching her from a distance, I'd force that upon myself as punishment for being what I was. The taste of her pussy would never be enough, but I would take as much as I could now to remember it for as long as I needed to until she let me touch her again.

Sliding off her panties, I cupped my hands under her ass to protect her delicate skin from the rough ground. She can be as tough as she wants, but she was still human, and I'd protect her as much as she'd allow me to. Her perfect pink pussy glistened with her arousal in the sunlight, and despite the warmth, she trembled, jumping and shrieking when I ran my tongue between her lips.

She tasted so fucking good.

Nikki's thighs clamped around my head as I

shoved my tongue into her pussy, nuzzling the soft nest of pubic hair with my nose before moving up and licking at her clit. Her grip on my hair was painful as she tugged me closer, pulling me into her while I licked and sucked, bringing her closer to the edge. I wanted to bring Nikki there, but I didn't want this to end, and all too soon she screamed out my name as she came with a flush over my lips and face, dripping down over my fingers.

Nikki was already grabbing at my arms and shoulders as her orgasm ebbed, and I moved over her, ready to claim her as mine. There were no words, no apologies or explanations, only the heat between us as I fumbled with my pants, freeing my cock before penetrating her, making Nikki cry out as I fully embedded myself in her slick warmth. Cradling Nikki against me, I protected her from the ground as much as I could. When she squeaked after a particularly rough thrust and was pushed painfully against a concrete edging, I picked her up with me and flipped over, sat on top of her father's grave, and pulled Nikki down onto my waiting cock.

She screamed, and her pussy clamped around me as my fingers dug into her hips. Leaning over me, she gripped the headstone as she rode me. She was wild, a demon unto herself, taking control and fucking down onto me. I didn't care that my thighs and ass were getting grazed and cut, the sweet pain only making the ecstasy of Nikki's hot cunt around my cock more intense.

Too soon I felt my release building, but I didn't want it to end. There was a finality in the air, a desperation to her movements, the way she ground and bounced against me. A violence and roughness to the touch that was an exacerbated version of who she is. Her eyes were closed, her mind full of too many betrayals and truths even I couldn't take away.

I needed to bring her to the edge with me.

Reaching between us, I flicked my finger across her clit, and her eyes snapped open, heavy with lust and pleasure, and lost in the moment. I found the perfect spot, rubbing in small tight circles until she was panting, her nails scraping against the stone of the grave behind my back as she brought herself off as well as me.

We came together, and I wrapped my arms around her, pulling her body close to mine, not ready to let her go.

CHAPTER
15

NIKKI

Cade's hold on me was almost painful, crushing my chest against his as a cool breeze licked at us.

Oh my God, we'd just had sex in a fucking graveyard.

What was I thinking? I wasn't, and that was the point. There was too much to think about, and I simply didn't want to think anymore. The chemistry between Cade and me pulled us together again, and I didn't want to fight it. Everything in my mind could wait because if this release could free me for even a short while, then I'd take it.

Cade's cock inside me was ecstasy, and he took me hard and fast before letting me ride him with the same vigor. There was nothing else even close to how he made me feel, and his hard chest pressing against my exposed breasts and my nipples rubbing against the fabric of his shirt was simply another sensation that drove me over the edge.

But as my high seeped away, all the thoughts returned, stronger and more persistent than before. I couldn't fuck away my problems, but it was worth a shot.

Lifting myself from Cade, his fingers tightened on my waist before he let me go, and I moved to collect my discarded clothes and cover up. Somehow, we'd not been caught, or perhaps if anyone had seen us, they'd decided they would rather not interrupt daylight fucking in a graveyard. Cade was watching me, his dark eyes following my movements until I stood in front of him, and he looked up at me. He was sitting in my shadow, the sun directly behind me so if I moved slightly to the side, he'd be temporarily blinded by the light, but he didn't look away, holding my gaze and evidently seeing nothing but me. After a moment, he pulled his pants up and covered himself. Here with the sunlight blazing down on both of us and without the distraction of the feel of his naked body under my hands and between my thighs, the moment we'd shared before was shattered.

Cade stood, and when he moved to embrace me, I stepped away from him. Something passed over his eyes, a darkness I had only seen in the moments before he fucked me, but then it was gone and replaced with the familiar pain behind his expression.

"How did you know my father?" I asked. I should have seen it the first time we came here, something like guilt had passed across his face when he had seen the picture on the gravestone, and naïvely, I assumed his guilt was because of my grieving because he didn't want me to hurt. What a joke.

Cade's jaw tensed as he gritted his teeth, but he said nothing for a moment, frowning as I crossed my arms over my chest. When he finally spoke up, and all he said was my name, I held up a hand.

"I don't want to hear excuses, Cade. I want the truth. Did you work together?"

Another pause, hesitation. Did he not feel he owed me the complete truth? "No."

"What then?"

"Nikki—"

"Cade!" I threw my arms up, and he flinched. "Tell me the fucking truth."

"I can't."

My jaw dropped. "I'm sorry, *what?*"

There was only sympathy on his face now, and I hated it. I didn't want him to feel *sorry* for me. I wanted him to tell me the truth, the full truth, and nothing but so I could finally move on with my life. Because now I had spent *years* searching for answers and found only more questions, and the man who could answer them for me stood right in front of me, feet planted firmly on top of dear old

Dad's grave, and he said he *couldn't* tell me.

"Can't or *won't?*" I said.

Cade closed his eyes for a moment, and I firmly shoved down the part of me that felt sorry for him because whatever internal battle he was fighting at this moment was his fault and not my problem. "I can't, Nikki. I'm sorry."

"You know what, Cade?" I moved forward, diving my hand into his jacket while he held his hands up, letting me rummage through his pockets. Finding the truck keys, I pulled them out and with everything I had, threw them across the graveyard. "Fuck you!"

The gravel crunched under my boots as I stormed away, and I refused to allow myself the luxury of turning around and seeing what I hoped was a stunned look on his gorgeous fucking face. I didn't want him to follow me to my car, trail me in his damn truck, or even worse, shove me in the back of his truck again under some bullshit excuse of protecting me.

Because he was just *too damn handsome*. His fucking words.

And because I didn't want him to see me cry.

Without work to distract me, I had nothing.

Even the lure of the investigation wasn't beaming as bright as it usually did. Because who was this man I was avenging? Now knowing that Urban was the hub of the business, I dove into research about the club for a while and found surprisingly little on it. There were more articles about minor drug busts from smaller clubs around the city than there were from Urban. It was almost *too clean.* But what did that tell me? Basically nothing. Because all I had to go on now was what people had told me, and I didn't feel like I could trust any of them. It felt like everyone had been lying to me about everything, and I didn't know who to believe.

Even the simple fact that I *doubted* my father's character bothered me. Why was I so ready to accept what Cade had told me? I'd known Dad for much longer than I knew Cade, so why take his word over family?

Because a voice in my head told me *there are too many things you ignored.*

Meetings with men who definitely *weren't* in real estate, accounting, or whatever other drivel I was sold. The gun I'd found in the drawer in his study that I'd never mentioned to anyone. That time he'd come home with what looked suspiciously like blood splatters on his clothes, which I readily believed was paint. The way he avoided photos being taken of him as best he could—really, I had none of him that I could recall. The ridiculous hours, the secrecy whenever there was a phone call.

Fuck, was I as blind, stupid, and naïve as the cops I'd been talking shit about?

Garrett—or Mitch, I didn't even know what to call him anymore—had invited me into his family as though I were his own daughter. Was I so taken with that, I was willing to forgive and even ignore a few missteps?

What I needed was proof, or at least the word of someone I trusted, and it didn't feel like there were many of those left. Snatching my cell from the kitchen counter, I typed out a text before dropping the phone and pacing, impatiently waiting for a response. Minutes later, it vibrated, buzzing across the counter in my otherwise silent home, and eagerly I grabbed it again.

Niles: *I'll come by in a couple of hours.*

It was the longest two and a half hours of my life, and when he knocked and I swung open the door, Niles swept my body with his gaze, not even bothering to hide the disapproval in his eyes.

"You look like hell," he said, stepping inside as I closed the door behind him.

"Thanks. Want a drink?"

"No, I can't stay."

"Good, because I just want to ask you a question, and I need honest information."

"Is this to do with Torres?"

I shook my head. I'd almost forgotten her, it seemed so long ago, a flicker of a happening that had been dampened by the tidal wave of information and doubt that plagued me now. Torres and Kim, victims of someone's *cleaning up house*, cutting loose ends and ties to this city.

Shit, why couldn't I think straight?

Was the mystery fucker trying to silence me simply to protect himself? It seemed obvious that would be his number one priority. But if he were after my father because of the business they were in and not the assets which Emrick admitted he had taken, then there were dangerous people involved.

This was sounding less and less like real estate, and every minute that passed felt like another dagger in my soul. I was falling apart at the seams and barely holding myself together because I didn't know who I was anymore. So long with a goal in sight only to have it slapped out from underneath me left me without stable footing and a whole world of questions I didn't have before.

"No," I sighed. *Did I really want to know?* Steeling myself, I finished, "I need you to tell me about Mitch Murphy."

Niles' shoulders tensed, and he shoved his hands in the pockets of his tan jacket, looking off to the side at nothing in particular while his jaw worked double time as though attempting to grind his teeth into stumps. "Why are you asking?"

Waving my hand dismissively, I pressed on. "Irrelevant. I need to know who he was."

"Tell me why, Nikki."

"I..." I licked my lips, realizing the irony of my next words, a direct reflection of what Cade had said to me. Cursing internally, I moved forward. I wasn't here to question Cade's motives or to think about him at all. "I can't tell you."

Niles stared hard at me, sighing before checking his watch and looking at me again. I could almost see the cogs in his mind turning, trying to figure out why I'd be asking about a man like Mitch Murphy, wondering if I was doing the opposite of instructed and investigating while suspended.

Of course, I fucking was. He knew me better than that.

"He disappeared years ago, and no one's heard from him since."

"And?"

Niles sighed again and looked at me like he wished he'd taken me up on my offer for a drink. "It's no secret this city is run by the crime syndicates that thrive underground. They have their fingers in everything and have control in almost all departments of law and justice."

I resisted the urge to reference my father's death

being signed off as a suicide when it was murder, not to mention Torres and Kim. Right now, Niles was giving me information he probably shouldn't, and burning that bridge would be a stupid idea.

"Murphy's territory was the largest," Niles continued, his discomfort visibly growing as the conversation progressed. "He was well protected and held a lot of influence. We could never get close to him, and there were so many contradicting reports on what he looked like, no one really knew for sure. He paid all the right people handsomely and not once had to answer for any of his crimes. If anything went down, he always had fall guys, and no matter how sweet the deal, no one would turn against him."

"What did he do?"

Niles lifted a shoulder. "What does anyone in that position do? Grow their empire and kill anyone who gets in their way. No amount of money is ever enough. The drug problem got so bad at one point the morale in the precincts was beyond abysmal, and there was a general *why bother* kind of attitude. We couldn't win."

"What happened?"

"He disappeared. There was a definitive shift in how the business was run, lower key, and bodies were no longer left displayed as a warning to others. I've no doubt the business is still running, but it's different now. No one has heard Murphy's name mentioned in years." He eyed me. "Until now."

I said nothing, letting the information wash over me while my expression remained impassive. This simply can't be true, and if Cade won't tell me *how* he knows these things he claims, how can I possibly trust him to be telling the truth? Emrick had no real reason to lie to me. It served no purpose to claim my father was someone he wasn't, he had his property before he was killed, and if all Dad did was worked in real estate, why would someone else then come along and kill him?

Revenge? Maybe to make sure he didn't build a new empire.

"Who were the other players?" I demanded.

"Nikki...."

"Niles, please, it's my last question, I promise." *For now.*

He sighed again and suddenly looked tired. "Vina and Rocko Sanchez, married couple. She used to be a stripper and married into the business. They own The Palace and most of the other major strip joints around here. As far as I'm aware, they don't engage in anything too nefarious, at least not on the surface, but they've cornered the strip and dance club market. They have connections, and no one messes with them."

"And?"

"And a few other smaller players, each battling for their own piece of the pie that's this shithole of a city. Murphy's biggest rival was Reuben Cole, and we know as much about him as we did Murphy."

My mouth went dry. "Do you think maybe Cole killed Murphy for his territory?"

"Perhaps, but without a body or evidence or any information, we can't prove that. What exactly was and wasn't Murphy's properties is unclear. He had them tied up in so many different names... Nikki, why are you asking this?"

"Was one of those names Garrett Porter?"

In the silence that followed, the air pounded against my eardrums insistently as I waited. "You can't be seriously suggesting..."

"I've recently come into some information that has indicated my father—"

"Nikki, no, that's not possible. Your father was a good man."

"How do you know that, Niles? Because of what I've told you? All the wonderful, heart-warming stories of how he took me in and loved me as though I were his own? Who's to say he didn't have other things going on I didn't know about? Wh-what?" I stammered as Nile's expression shifted.

My resistance was breaking, shattering down faultlines through my body from too much doubt, fear, and heartbreak all at once. "What does that look mean, Niles? Do you think if we look up his history that it'll be squeaky clean, and that will help me? What if it's *too clean*? I know because I already did it when I first started investigating his death. There's nothing, *nothing,* in his history to indicate criminal activity, not even a fucking parking ticket. The man was so clean I'm beginning to wonder if the identity was the front I'm being told it was."

Niles grabbed my shoulders, and I twisted to get out of his grip, but he held tight. "Nikki, you *must* let this go. It's tearing you apart, can't you see? I don't know who put these ideas in your head, but it's not possible."

"You don't know that." Resignation was heavy in my tone, and Niles' hands dropped from my arms. He knew it too. There was no way to know for sure. Murphy was too good, covering his tracks every way he went, to the point that no one even knew if he was dead or not.

But you know, don't you, Nikki?

The voices in my head were torturing me, and even though Niles sat me on the couch and made me a cup of tea before leaving, and I assured him I was fine and would drop it, I knew he didn't believe my words any more than I did. I was plagued simultaneously by too much information and not enough. The law enforcement had been paid off for too long, there was no evidence, no records, and even if there were, I had no way to access them. No one would talk to me, and it's a fucking miracle I got to talk to Emrick at all and received that little clue.

But that one little clue led me down this path of

self-destruction. Destruction of everything I thought I knew about who my father was and subsequently, about who I was and what I was even doing with my life. If the criminal syndicates were that rampant in this city, what was the point in even trying? They had control over everything, and the police were simply going through the motions, pretending we could make a difference in a city we had already lost.

I was caught in a spiral that was consuming me, and there was nowhere to go but down.

CHAPTER 16

CADE

When in full demon form, the glowing red outline of the pentagram would display on my chest, a branding of my species that never faded or waivered and glowed as brightly as the lines of demonic power that traced their way across my naturally black skin. A tapestry of our age and family history, and every demon's markings were different. For those who had bonded and broken those bonds, they'd be left with large welts across their skin. A darker crimson cut around their torso, arms, and neck as though the invisible ropes that had bound them to their partner were dragged over their body until it burned a permanent reminder into them of the promise they had broken.

Demons didn't take bonding with their life partners lightly.

Entry and exit to Hell weren't particularly difficult if you held the marking and knew the incantations, and human souls didn't take the same path we did to move between realms. We were living, breathing beings, not souls passing across after death. They slid from one realm to another as though passing through water, and many weren't aware they had died if it were a peaceful death. But demons must open a gate to Hell, and despite mythology, there wasn't *a* single gate to Hell but many, almost anywhere we needed them to be.

You needed wings to move to Heaven and the marking to move to Hell.

After months of keeping my human form and denying my demon, the shift didn't come easy, but it was helped along by the rage and guilt that burned in my system and flowed through my veins. The desire to either fight my way to feeling better or to claim Nikki again was intense, a need that I feared would now be denied forevermore.

The eyes were the first to change, always becoming yellow with black slits for irises. Yellow eyes were the first sign of a demon losing control or someone intentionally allowing their demon loose from within. Then bones cracked and crunched, and I crouched in an alley, hidden by the buildings and the darkness of night. Blackness exploded from my veins like ink, flooding my skin and changing my complexion to an almost impossible black, which started in blotches until they spread like spider webs and cascaded across my skin, reaching for each other and joining, covering me in the dark color. The markings came next, red and bright, glowing with the light of demonic power and weaving their way across my skin before finally making their way to my chest and carving out the pentagram that would allow my access to Hell.

My hair disappeared, my teeth and nails grew sharp, and my clothes shredded as the ridges grew on my back, shoulders, elbows, calves, and ankles. Hook-like appendages that were only good for bloodshed. Breathing ragged and rasping against my rough throat, serrated with barbs that allowed prey to be swallowed whole but not be drawn back up, I stood and shook my limbs out. They felt long and uncomfortable, and I much preferred my human form. But even if I could move to Hell as a human, I wouldn't make it far before I was questioned. I didn't yet have a plan on how to explain my absence for the past few months. Leaving Hell for Earth meant I didn't have to explain myself, but going back opened up questions.

But I had to.

This was important.

This was for Nikki.

The incantation was spoken in our demonic language, and I muttered it under my breath, waiting for the heat to rise from under my feet, the welcoming pit where flames licked up the side for dramatic effect before I dropped down. Landing on my feet in the stone cavern, I made my way through the maze of brimstone and magma, and despite all the things I hated about this place, the comforting warmth tingled pleasantly against my skin, and it was nice to relinquish all control and be in my natural form, even if for a short while as I walked. I encountered no one along the way, although I had no doubt they knew I was there.

Taking a few shortcuts and cutting through hidden crevices in the stone walls, I found Murphy naked and strung up on a giant wooden X-frame, designed after the one he used to torture his victims on Earth when he wanted information. No matter what he had been through, Murphy's soul form hadn't lost that look of irony in his eyes. He understood exactly why he was here and seemed to have accepted his fate. He'd never once begged me to stop, not while I was doing the torturing, though I suspected now another demon had taken over that may change. They were crueler than I.

"What now?" Murphy spat, staring at me through one eye, the other swollen shut and the side of his face bloody. Physical torture worked best for men like Murphy, but psychological torment only worked if they felt guilt. "You gonna tear my balls off and make me eat them again?"

Again? Fuck, that wasn't one of mine.

"I'm not here to torture you. I have questions."

His expression changed at my voice, and while I had correctly assumed he wouldn't be able to tell demons apart from one another, apparently he recognized me now.

"Oh, it's you. Well, that is a pity. You did have a softer touch than the others."

I scowled at him but didn't argue.

"You'll answer my questions and ask none of your own." Murphy's eyes narrowed, but he said nothing and waited for me to speak again. I had come here for a specific reason, but now that he was in front of me again, I was tied up with Nikki, and there was something else playing in the back of my mind I wanted answers to. "You're a cruel man, Mitch," I said.

"Was that your question, or are you working up to it?"

Snarling again, I was pleased to see him flinch, if only slightly, at my display of aggression. "Tell me… why would a man like you dote on a stepdaughter so much?"

His demeanor changed instantly, and in a few seconds, he worked through a world of conflicting emotions—confusion, fear, anger, regret, remorse, and anger again. If I were a darker being, I'd tell the others that I'd found something Murphy feels guilty about, a button they could push over and over to torture him without laying a hand on him. But I didn't want Nikki or Murphy's memory of her used in that way.

"Who are you?"

"You know me," I growled out. "We've spent a lot of quality time together. Now answer my question."

"Why are you asking about her? How do you know these things?" Panic was edging in his tone. He wanted to know, but he didn't want to risk giving me additional information.

He was still protecting her.

Why?

"I want to know why you treated her as you did. She seemed to be the only exception, except, I assume, for your wife. Nikki has nothing but glowing memories of you and adores you to this day, yet hundreds, maybe thousands of others would condemn you to death for what you've done. So tell me *why.*"

"I'm not telling you *shit!*"

I couldn't let Murphy know that this line of questioning was unusual, that demons don't question their victims. If we want to know something from a human, we cut them and drink their blood, allowing the offering of their darkest memories to fill us with fuel we can use against them.

I smiled, knowing it showed the sharpness of my teeth and made my yellow eyes glint and glow in a way that made humans' skin crawl. I chuckled. "I've been on the surface, I know Nikki. She's quite an attractive woman. Maybe I'll—"

"You stay the *fuck* away from her!"

The smirk was still on my face as I watched him. Should I tell him I had already fucked her? More than once? No, that was between her and me, and my lip lifted in a possessive snarl at even the idea of someone else thinking of her the way I do.

"Does it torture you?" I snarled, making sure I was close enough he could feel the heat from my skin. "To know I was with her?"

His teeth were bared as he pushed out the word, "*Yesss,*" ending in a hiss.

"Then I'm still doing my duty."

I didn't tell him that it tortured me too.

Murphy's forehead was slick with sweat, and panic was etched into his usually hard expression. The idea of a demon so close to his daughter was driving him crazy, but I wasn't leaving until I found out his reasons. He wasn't the saint she thought he was for all these years.

"Tell me," I snarled, letting the words draw out into an otherworldly growl that had him trembling in his shackles.

He closed his eyes for a moment, and when he opened them, his expression was stony again, fighting to keep control in a game where he had no leverage. "When I met Yasmin, we were very young, back before I even knew what the family business was."

I said nothing but didn't fight to keep my expression neutral. The frown that was adorning my face made Murphy flinch again. But it wasn't anger, it was confusion. Nikki had said Murphy and her mother, Yasmin, were only married a few years. Now he was talking about her like they were together since they were young.

"She was my first love, and I was hers. But when I got into the business, I cut ties with her, not wanting her to be involved." Murphy looked away from me, and I approached, grabbing his face and digging my claws into his skin when he didn't speak again straightaway.

I was done waiting. "Talk."

"We met again years later, and feelings I'd forgotten I could feel came flooding back. She had Nikki, and she said she'd had her with another man. But the timing... there was that one night we'd seen each other after the split... and Nikki's eyes..." Murphy looked at me with hazel eyes I hadn't paid much attention to before, and my stomach churned. "I think Nikki was mine. But even if she wasn't, she was like a little angel. I lied to her and her mother about what I did. Even the name she knew me by when we were young wasn't real. Yasmin never knew. I was schooled under one name, worked under another, and conducted business as who I was. I told Yasmin I changed my name to distance myself from a cruel father and claimed Garrett was my name now. Yasmin loved me, but she was naïve, and she didn't question me much. We only had a few years together anyway."

Murphy scowled, and I returned the look, feeling the waves of emotion coming from him. "My son, born from a one-night stand who didn't want him, was dropped at my doorstep at age seven, shortly after I first left Yasmin. How the slut found me, I can only fucking guess. Maybe her family was in the same business as mine, but I never found out her last name, so I couldn't give him back. He knew who I really was. He resented Nikki, but he was a dark boy, and perhaps I made that worse with how I treated him. When he hit nineteen, he got worse, like there was an evil living within him, and even by my standards, he was violent."

He lifted a shoulder, and his indifference to how he treated his own child made my skin crawl. "He wanted to sell Nikki when she turned eighteen and her mother, my Yasmin, was gone. Nikki was beautiful as she grew, and she looked innocent. Someone would pay a hefty price for her as a slave, he said, or perhaps to use as a bargaining chip to sweeten a deal. I cut him from the business and my life, and that was a couple of years before I was killed."

He looked at me then, his expression hard. "I don't dispute that I deserved to die, but I always assumed it would be *for* my business. That fucker, Emrick, found out about my family, about Nikki, and threatened them after what he did to me…" He tilted his head, indicating his missing ear. "I have no doubt he'd have followed through with his promises. He left me alive, but without the protection of my business and with the enemies I had made, I was easy pickings."

"Who killed you?" I whispered. His eyes widened, his jaw dropped, and I waited for him to utter a name that would end Nikki's suffering. A large, clawed hand landed on my shoulder, and I dropped my grip from Murphy's face as another hand gripped my arm.

I knew I shouldn't have asked, but I had to try.

It wasn't up to demons to seek revenge nor bring murderers to justice until they were in our realm. The question I had just asked was not taken lightly, and as I was dragged away, Murphy shouted out to me. "You stay the fuck away from her! You hear me?"

I wanted to laugh in his face because I'd never stay away from Nikki. But a demon stood in front of Murphy before slashing its claws across his chest, a waterfall of blood dripping down over his naked body before he was gone from my sight. The demons dragging me away said nothing, and I didn't struggle. While I hadn't gotten the information I came here to get, I had found out more than I thought I would. If I hadn't been so selfish and asked the most important question first, perhaps I'd have gotten away with it and had my answers before I was caught.

Because I was always going to be caught, I knew that.

But no, I needed to know so desperately why she was special. She may have been his *actual* daughter, and while it shouldn't make a lick of fucking difference to how you treat a child, stepchild, or otherwise, it ignited some long-forgotten, old-fashioned father protectiveness in Murphy. But this didn't erase all the other things he had done, the people he had killed, and the lives destroyed in his pursuit of more power and money. Not to mention the way he had treated his son as a second-class citizen, exactly as his father had treated him before, and on and on, creating a cycle of abuse.

Where was his son now? I didn't know. Perhaps he is running his own business, following in the footsteps of his father, not knowing any other way to live.

To suggest *selling* Nikki as a teenager, he was just as sick as Murphy.

Dragged into a chamber, my arms were lifted above my head and shackled to the warm stone wall with heavy restraints. I didn't try to struggle, knowing this would happen.

Banishment from Hell can only be achieved by

destroying the pentagram etched into the skin on my chest. Incantations would be needed, and while the pentagram could be destroyed simply by breaking the outline, cutting and scarring me, that wasn't enough for them.

Demons took pleasure in the pain of others, and they would make sure it would be more excruciating than necessary to get the job done.

But for Nikki, for what I had done and who I was, I'd take it all.

This was what it felt like to repent.

CHAPTER
17

NIKKI

Two days since the graveyard, Cade simply showed up on my doorstep. He must have walked, for I didn't hear the tell-tale rumble of the truck pulling up and the tires hitting the sidewalk as he parked so as not to block the narrow street. But the knock on the door was followed almost immediately by Cade calling my name, and I debated leaving him out in the rain.

His knocking was persistent, and I peeled myself off the couch, placing my almost empty beer on the coffee table before making my way to the door. I stared at the heavy old wooden slab that stood between Cade and me for too long, and he knocked again.

The second I had unlocked the deadbolt, he turned the handle, pushing the door inward and falling into the small foyer. I thought he was drunk and was ready on the precipice of rolling my eyes until I saw the blood.

Dropping to my knees. I rolled him over onto his back and cried out, slapping my hand over my mouth. His face was pale, his shirt almost soaked through with blood, and I prayed the rain had exacerbated the effect, soaking the fabric of his T-shirt and spreading what I hoped was a misleadingly small amount of blood. Even as I watched, the fabric darkened, spots continuing to flow, indicating a large wound beneath, centered on his chest. His arms were also covered in cuts, but while they were congealing as he healed, the chest wound was something else.

"Fuck, Cade, what happened to you?" I whispered.

He simply groaned, and his eyes opened blearily before he looked at me, a world of pain and regret behind those eyes. I bit my lip. I was mad at the guy, but I didn't want him to suffer like this. *Oh, please, Cade, tell me this isn't some self-inflicted punishment.* Cade groaned again when I moved him and protested when I tried to drag him to his feet. "Please help me, Cade. I need you on the couch so I can treat your wound."

"Don't look," he muttered, the words slurred and whispered, barely making it past his lips.

"What?"

But he didn't speak again and, with a herculean effort, pushed himself to his feet, leaning his weight heavily on my shoulder as I steered him toward the couch. I barely made it without my legs buckling under his weight, and he fell back against it. Cade didn't protest as I removed his shoes and heaved his legs onto the couch so he was lying. Muttering a stream of curses, my head started to ache when I jumped to my feet. Days of drowning my sorrows in beer was catching up with me when I needed to have a clear head, and I forced myself to concentrate before running to the bathroom to grab the first-aid kit.

Kneeling back next to Cade, he weakly swatted my hands away as I tried to lift his shirt. "If you didn't want my help, why did you come here?" I snapped, pushing his hands away so I could peel the blood-soaked fabric from him. Cursing again, I grabbed some scissors and cut the T-shirt from his body, peeling it back to reveal his chest.

Fucking hell, Cade.

Large triangular cuts were sliced into his chest, and my stomach churned as I realized the skin had been peeled back before being replaced. They were not clean cuts, and if they weren't done with a serrated knife, he was torn apart by an animal. But the placement was too calculated to be a wildlife attack. Minor wounds I'd treated, but this… this was something else entirely.

"Cade." I swallowed against the lump in my throat. "Cade, you need to go to the hospital."

He was pale, his eyes closed and sweat glistening on his forehead, his hands and nails were covered in blood, and I wondered if it was his own from trying to stem the flow of blood or if he had fought against whoever did this. "No hospital."

"Cade, *please,* you need stitches, and I don't have the tools or the expertise. Let me call an ambulance."

"No stitches. No hospital."

Tears prickled against the back of my eyes as a wave of helplessness rushed over me. Slapping my cheek lightly to bring myself into line, I steeled my nerves. No hospital? Then I'd just need to do the best I could. He wasn't in my good books at the moment, but that didn't mean I would let him bleed to death.

Although, this might be a good opportunity to ask some questions.

Did that make me an asshole, taking advantage of his weakened state like that? Maybe. But I'd done nothing but wallow in my own self-pity and loathing for the past few days, and I'd had enough. I needed to get back on track and figure out what I was going to do next. I needed to know how Cade knew the things he claimed to be true.

Wiping the blood away with paper towels, Cade hissed through his teeth every time I passed over the exposed wound not covered by the jagged remains of his skin. I told him to brace himself because this was going to hurt like hell, and he made a sound that almost seemed like a chuckle before I sprayed the antiseptic over his chest. Cade snarled at me, and I flinched, the sound so animalistic it caught me off guard.

"I think I need to stitch the skin back together..." I had no idea. Basic first-aid training didn't cover *this.* Cade shook his head, his body trembling with the effort.

"Will heal," he whispered.

Dabbing down the side of his ribs to dry off the excess antiseptic as it dripped toward the couch, I asked, "When did you know who my father was?"

The frown on Cade's forehead deepened, but he didn't move or look at me as he answered, each word an effort. "When I saw his picture on the gravestone."

I huffed out a sigh, biting my tongue against reprimanding him for not telling me sooner. While I understood his reasons—he claimed to care about me and didn't want to hurt me—the way the information had come out cut deeply. The fact I couldn't seem to verify it one way or the other was only twisting the knife.

"How did you know him?" He didn't answer, so I pushed forward. "Did you work together? You said you liked to fight. Were you some sort of a gun-for-hire or something?"

"I'm not a violent being." Cade's voice was strained, but I was finding it difficult to summon any additional sympathy. He owed me answers.

Slapping the gauze pad over his chest, probably harder than necessary, Cade growled again. "Then *what?*" I hissed out, glaring at him, "Did you run drugs? Were you his goddamn receptionist? Did you go out on the pull together, you as his wingman? *What?*"

Cade had started trembling again, the sign of weakness from his body in stark contrast to the hardness of his expression. His face had gone blank and cold, and he was keeping his eyes shut, probably so he didn't have to look at me and face the truth. I placed a hand gently over the gauze on his chest, my other hand clenched around the bandages. I'd need him to sit up to wrap it, but right now, I couldn't draw my eyes away from his.

Under his eyelids, his pupils were darting wildly around as though he were asleep and having a nightmare.

"Cade?" I prompted.

I was pushing him.

I knew it was wrong, but I couldn't stop.

I had to know.

"I only met your father a year ago."

Confusion welled up in my gut, churning quickly with the stomach acid and creating anger. "What?

What are you *talking* about? He died three years ago!"

Now his lip was twitching, every motion exposing his teeth more.

I had never noticed his teeth were sharp before. How did I not notice that?

When he didn't speak, I scoffed. "Please don't tell me you think you're some sort of psychic medium or something." *Nothing.* "If you come back to me with that... if *all of this* is because of some *vision* you had or some bullshit, I'm going to blow my fucking top."

"I met him in *Hell.*"

Numbness washed over my limbs, and now I didn't even know *what* I felt. Pushing myself away from the couch, I stood, pacing the room. "You better start making sense *right fucking now,* Cade, or I swear to God—"

"You *swear...*"

My back was to him when the words came, but it wasn't Cade, not the Cade I knew. The voice was darkness in a soundwave that drifted through the air and touched my eardrums, sending shivers cascading down my spine. Dropping the bandage, I ducked my chin against my chest, my shoulders trembling. I didn't want to turn around and see why he had spoken in such a voice that sounded as though it consisted of two tones at once. I didn't want to know what the cracking I heard was or why it sounded like his clothes were being shredded from his body.

The wall in front of me was obscured by a shadow larger than the man I had left on the couch.

Heart thumping a drum beat in my chest, I slowly turned around.

CHAPTER
18

CADE

It wasn't news to me that I was weak.

I was weak in Hell, unable to be enough of a demon to earn the respect of others. Then when I came to Earth, I thought that would change until my weakness was exposed all over again in the form of a human I cared about—Nikki. I simply couldn't keep myself from seeing her, even though I knew she probably needed some space, if she wanted to see me again at all. None of that was enough to keep me from her front door when I was in pain as the wounds inflicted to destroy my pentagram healed slowly. Beyond the physical pain was the emotional torment that plagued me, guilt that cut deeper than the claws that had shredded the skin on my chest. Every step I had taken had only made things harder for Nikki when all I wanted to do was release her from her burdens.

I was weak.

And I was too weak to keep my demon form contained when all the pain came to the surface. When the physical and emotional trauma rose, I had to grit my teeth and clench my jaw against the feeling that I was being attacked from the inside, a thousand dangers working their way through my heart, lungs, and gut.

Once the transformation started, I couldn't stop it, and my shoulders shook with the pain of seeing Nikki there, her back to me, trembling with the adrenaline that ran through her body. She was reacting to the sounds and sense of me, feelings she couldn't explain. Darkness and foreboding filled her home that can only be brought on by the presence of a demon.

I should have run before she turned around, but the pain was still tearing through my body, shooting up and down my limbs and settling the heaviest on my chest. The transformation, additionally painful because I continued to fight it, had ripped open the wounds that had only begun healing, and the red lines of demonic power that marked my skin blurred into the blood that stained my chest.

I didn't think I'd ever be able to erase from my mind the terror in her eyes when she saw me.

There wasn't a scream, no sound escaped her,

although her mouth fell open as though she wanted to. All the terror was caught in her throat, and only a weak squeak escaped, a murmur of not understanding.

Leave, my mind was screaming at me. *Run before you do any more damage.*

"I'm sorry," I said in this form, unable to control the sound of my voice. She flinched at the tone, all gravel, fire, and darkness wrapped together with an ethereal quality.

"C-Cade?" The stuttered whisper shattered my already broken heart, and when I reached for her, Nikki flinched again, wrapping her arms around her chest and backing against the opposite wall. I dropped my hand, the claws and barbs making me sick simply to look at myself.

Still, I felt I needed to explain. I couldn't leave her like this. "Your father wasn't a good man, and in the afterlife, he came to me." Nikki squeaked out a weak protest, even faced with me in my true form, her streak of stubbornness made itself known. "I'm sorry," I said it again but knew the words would never be enough. "I wish things had been different."

There was nothing I could do to comfort her. The best thing right now would be to get away from her so she can heal and move on. Hell, I shouldn't have even come to her home in the first place. With a roar of rage and pain that had Nikki sliding down the wall until she was tucked into the corner, I stalked out of her home and sprinted down the street.

I needed to find somewhere dark and private to ride out these emotions until I could change back again.

NIKKI

How long I stayed curled up in the corner like a child, I don't really know. There was no whirlwind of thoughts running through my mind and no connections being made of all the things I'd found out recently.

In my mind, there was simply nothing.

Because all the space was occupied by the repeating visions of the man I knew as Cade, turning into a terrifying beast and standing before me, apologizing for what he had done, for what he was.

Skin darker than the space between stars, darker than the corner in your room that seems to haunt you at night, teasing the presence of a monster you can't see. Skin lined with red tattoos that traced across his body in intricate patterns that would be almost beautiful if it weren't for how they all led to his chest, now a bloodied mess.

But the eyes, the yellow eyes with black slits for pupils, were like a cat's or some creature from a horror movie. Why did I feel like I could still see

Cade behind those eyes? That was impossible. Although he was in that monster somewhere, he was no longer Cade.

And never would be again.

In the afterlife, he came to me.

Had I fucked the *Devil?*

Eventually, I lifted myself to my feet, my arm shaking as I supported myself against the wall, my body burdened and heavy with dread and confusion. Lurching forward, I stumbled into the kitchen and dropped to my knees, searching the cupboards, barely keeping the contents of my stomach where they should be. There had to be something here, something I could numb my mind with. Because after the period of emptiness, all the thoughts were coming back now, each fighting for a position at the front and demanding to be sorted.

Hell exists. Heaven and Hell. My father was a bad man. He went to Hell. He met Cade there. What of the man who killed him and threatened me? Was he even human? Did Cade know who he was? Should I keep trying to find the murderer? The truth always comes out. If this was the truth, I didn't want it. But I needed to find justice. For who? Me? My father? I never even knew him.

I sobbed, biting the inside of my cheek to stop the sound.

Did anything even matter anymore?

With a sigh of relief, I wrapped my fingers

around the dusty glass neck of the whiskey bottle. I hated whiskey, which was why the gifted bottle after my graduation from the academy remained untouched in the cupboard. But right now, I needed something, *anything,* to stop the thoughts. I didn't want to think or feel, and when I cracked open the lid, I ignored the smell that made my nose scrunch as I raised the bottle to my lips and took half a dozen grateful mouthfuls of the liquid.

Barely avoiding dropping the bottle, I leaned back against the opposite cupboard and coughed against the burn in my throat. Apparently, aging cheap whiskey does nothing to improve it.

I drank. Not caring that I hadn't eaten in a while and that my aversion to dark spirits meant my tolerance was low. I simply kept drinking. After a short while, the press of the cupboard handle in between my shoulder blades was nothing more than a memory, and my eyelids started to droop.

Eventually, I'd pass out, and then tomorrow, I would have enough whiskey left to keep me numb until I made it to the liquor store, thankfully within walking distance. I had the urge to drive to the graveyard to see my father because I wasn't sure if I wanted to scream at the ground and simply hope his spirit in Hell below his rotting body in the soil could hear me or if I wanted to punch at the gravestone until my knuckles bled. Maybe I'd take my new best friends, in the shape of bottles of numbing goodness, with me and continue this stupor.

How long could I go on like this?

It didn't matter.

I couldn't even think about dealing with this shit now or any time soon.

I had just enough awareness left to put the bottle down before I dropped it, as my vision slowly grayed from the edges, moving inward until the entire room felt like it was rolling around me.

Maybe I'd choke on my vomit and die while unconscious.

Then I'd see Cade and Hell, and he could explain to me why he ruined my life.

CHAPTER
19

CADE

Frank was fed up with my attitude before the phone call had ended. He usually treated me with a certain level of humor, being as I was younger and, therefore, arguably more immature than him. Granted, I had called him when I already had too much shit going on in my head, and I'd practically shouted at him when he tried to make small talk.

All I needed to know was when he was next at the fight club.

Tonight.

Since the horrific encounter with Nikki yesterday, I hadn't slept, eaten, or rested at all. It had taken hours for the emotions to get to a point where I could stabilize them enough to change back into my human form, and I hadn't tried to keep inside the howls of agony and heartache that escaped my already aching throat. The wound on my chest had almost healed, although I was now left with scars that vaguely resembled a pentagram and looked as though I'd been attacked with a rusty sword over it. These scars wouldn't go away, not even in my human form. They would be there to forever remind me of my betrayal and that I could never go home.

I didn't want to go back, but there was a difference between making that decision myself and having the decision taken from me.

I could only hope Nikki was coping okay, and I doubted my presence would be of any comfort to her, so there was no point in rocking up at her home and trying to talk it out. Not right away, at least. But I wasn't going to give up on her.

She was mine.

The guilt and rage were pounding through my veins, and I paced around the warehouse for hours before demons began showing up. Several of them challenged me to a fight, but I ignored them. They were not worth my time. I needed Frank and only Frank. I needed the kind of instinct that could only be drawn out by fighting my kin, and he was bigger and stronger than most.

Frank strolled into the warehouse with the same suave smugness as he would a business meeting, and he stripped his jacket and white shirt off casually, tossing them over a dusty and crumbling bench before coming to face me. I hadn't stopped moving, shifting between impatient pacing and bouncing on my feet, clenching and unclenching my hands, and stripped down to my pants and tank.

Frank circled me cautiously, a deep frown embedded between his dark brows. He rubbed at the stubble on his chin as he studied me. "Are you okay, brother?"

I snorted. "No talking."

His eyebrow arched, and he shrugged a shoulder before he closed the gap between us in a handful of large strides, hooked an arm over my neck, and forced me to bend before he drove a punch into my nose. I cried out in rage and fought against his hold. No longer burdened with the etiquette of correct fighting practice, I simply allowed myself to become an animal. Thrashing against Frank, he let me go more out of surprise than strength, and I used his hesitation against him, snatching his arm and twisting it behind his back. Frank was forced to his knees, and his eyes flared yellow as his rage took over. He didn't know why I was fighting dirty, nor what caused the change between the last time we fought and now.

But he didn't need to know.

All I wanted from him to be sure of was there were no limits anymore and for him to fight me without holding back.

I cried out when he reached back and drove his

fingers into my calf, letting only his hands change so his claws drove into my skin, and I let him go. As Frank stood and we faced each other, I snarled at him as his hand returned to human form, and I failed to keep my rage at his perfect control of his demon at bay. "No demon forms, aren't those the rules?"

"I don't know what the fuck your problem is, Cade, but something tells me the rules are out the window." His eyes traveled my body, and when they came to rest on my chest, they widened. Ignoring my warning growls and subsequent roar of rage, he reached forward and snatched at my tank, ripping downward and shredding it from my body.

"Oh, Cade," he whispered, eyeing the scars on my chest. "What did you do?"

Launching at him, he stepped forward to meet my attack, and we met shoulder to shoulder, bent at the waist, and wrestled each other for power. When I landed a few punches to his gut, Frank snarled and returned the favor. The power behind his blows brought to the surface a realization that he had been pulling his punches last time we met like this.

And that only served to increase my anger.

Layers upon layers of rage, hatred, and guilt were within me until I was nothing but a culmination of all the negative emotions that made me the worst of mankind and still not dark enough to be demon either.

I should never have gotten involved with Nikki.

I should never have tried to help.

And I should never have let my touch be anything more than a fuck and release.

When the vision of her hazel eyes floated in front of my memory, her pale skin with slightly pink cheeks, her freckles, and white-blonde hair, I roared again. The vision faded and changed until I was looking into those same hazel eyes, but now it was Murphy, laughing and mocking me. Changing my stance, I got hold of Frank and lifted him over my shoulder before slamming him onto the floor.

There was a resounding *ooh* of appreciation from the crowd that had gathered, but I didn't care about them. Frank was on his feet, covered in dirt and dust, and his shoulder was sliced by a stray piece of broken glass.

And the look in his eyes was pure rage.

"What *is* this?" he asked. "Are you *trying* to piss me off?"

"Yes," I growled out.

It wasn't strictly true, as that wasn't what I came here for. But when he asked, I realized that ultimately making Frank as angry as me *was* my goal. Because if Frank felt like I did, he might just kill me.

"What are you punishing yourself for?" Frank said, frowning at me.

Somehow, he had hit me right in my most vulnerable spot with the question, and there was no way I would admit it. That was a line of questioning I wasn't interested in exploring right now, and I responded by running at him again. Expertly, Frank countered my attack, forcing me to my knees and standing behind me, one arm wrapped around my throat and holding onto his wrist, choking me against the crook of his elbow.

"Cade." His voice was calm again, and I hated it. "Stop."

"No, I need this."

Frank snarled when I bit into his arm, letting me go as I drew blood. He shot me a look of such hatred that, for a split second, I doubted myself. Then it all came flooding back, and that moment was gone, lost in the rush of emotion that threatened to crush me.

So, I let it all go.

I don't recall all the details of the fight. Every ounce of energy that wasn't directed at keeping my human form, I threw into the fight, somehow making Frank the object of all my pain, and if only I could bring him down, then I'd feel better. I almost succeeded, and when we were both bloodied and beaten, Frank sporting a black eye which he'd roared, *"Not the face!"* at me when I'd given it to him, and the wound on my chest reopened when he clawed me again, we backed away from each other.

Panting, we watched each other wearily, Frank

looking mildly shell-shocked that I'd been able to inflict so much damage. "Are you ready to talk about it?"

"Fuck you," I spat out.

Frank simply raised his brows at me, straightening as he lifted his shoulder in another half-shrug after rolling them. "Suit yourself. Do you want to keep going?"

I thought I did, but after the past hour, now that we had stopped, I felt drained and numb inside. I was happy to not be feeling an avalanche of emotions anymore, but I didn't like this feeling of hollow nothingness. Nikki returned to my thoughts as if she was ever far from them, and the nothingness was replaced with an ache that swallowed my heart.

Gritting my teeth against the tears welling behind my eyes, I squeezed my eyes shut as I heard Frank sigh and approach. "Let me give you a ride home, you stupid fuck."

Sighing to myself, it was as close to a term of endearment as I was going to get from him. "Okay."

Of course, he drove some expensive European car,

and I shuffled in my seat, aware that I was probably getting blood on the cream upholstery. Frank was too, but he didn't seem to care, but then again, it was his expensive car, and he could do with it as he wished.

Part of me wondered if he purchased the expensive vehicles and suits to keep up appearances or if he genuinely enjoyed the luxury. I suspected a bit of both but could barely form any thoughts, let alone ask a coherent question and maintain a conversation. Frank was hardly the sort for pointless conversation anyway, and I'd never been more thankful for that than right now.

"Do you want to talk about what happened?" he asked after a while.

"No."

Frank pursed his lips and nodded, keeping his eyes firmly on the road. His grip on the steering wheel tightened until his knuckles turned white. "How did you lose your mark?"

"I said I don't want to talk about it."

"I don't really give a shit what you want, *parvulus puer*. You're too wrapped up with this human woman, and it's not good for you."

"Don't talk about her."

"First, you try to solve a murder for her, now I'm guessing by your scars..." Frank threw an indignant look at my chest before returning his gaze to the road, illuminated by LED headlights, "... you went back home to ask something you shouldn't, of someone you *definitely* shouldn't be talking to."

"Drop it, Frank."

"What happened? Were you desperate to know something about some past fuck-buddy of hers? Maybe find out her kinks? Why you can't make her come?"

There was screaming of tires and a responsive angry hail of horns as Frank's car swerved dangerously into the oncoming lane. His eyes flared yellow as he corrected the vehicle, and he rubbed his jaw, glaring at me as I retreated to my seat, rubbing my knuckles.

"I'm going to forgive that punch..." he muttered, frowning, "... provided there are no scratches on my fucking car."

"Just leave it alone. Please."

He threw me one last look before sighing loudly. "Fine." Pressing a button on his steering wheel, the radio flared to life, and he switched back and forth between two stations—Nine Inch Nails on one and something that sounded like Mozart. I watched his face as he decided between the two, the decision seeming to tear him. By the time he settled on Nine Inch Nails, the song was almost over, and we were pulling up to the front of my apartment building.

I expected him to keep the car idling and drop me off, but he stopped the car. Getting out and striding around the vehicle, Frank grabbed my arm as I went to leave. "Cade."

"What?"

"She's human." I simply grunted in response, and Frank's brow furrowed, his fists clenching. He was ready to fight over the point if I was going to push it. "Let her go."

"No."

Frank stared at me again, his fingers flexing before his shoulders dropped in resignation, and he held out his hand. I took it to shake, and his grip increased with a move I was too distracted to see coming as he landed a punch to my nose, using his grip on my hand to yank me back toward him and keep me standing. I snarled at him, which he ignored. "That's for punching me while driving, asshole." As he turned to leave, he paused before getting back into the driver's seat. "I care about you, brother," he said, tapping his fingers on the roof of his car. "I'm only trying to help."

"I *know*," I snarled before sighing and reducing my voice to a whisper, humbled by a show of affection from a demon such as Frank. "I know."

Frank watched me for a beat, his expression unreadable. "Go to bed, Cade."

Waking up the next morning was trying, and it was only through my loyalty to Smithy that I bothered at all. According to Frank, no humans were worth our loyalty, but if I couldn't save Nikki, I could at least help Smithy out. Sliding from the bed, I followed my morning routine, hoping that the simple acts would return some feeling of normality. Slowly, I was accepting nothing was going to make me forget Nikki, especially not physical pain, and the idea of other women wasn't something I could even consider now. Although, in order to keep my demon under control, eventually, I'd have to. Maybe distance would help—find another city to inhabit and make a semblance of a home, or maybe I'd drift from place to place.

Going home to Hell was no longer an option, but I hardly cared about that.

The look in her eyes when she saw me still haunted me, and it was all I saw when I closed my eyes and tried to sleep last night.

Flicking on the television to the morning news, I strode to the kitchenette and stared into the almost empty refrigerator. Nothing was appetizing.

Looking ahead at the weather, it's going to be a humid one today, up to seventy-two percent in some areas. There may be a drizzle in the afternoon to accompany this...

Oh good, gloomy weather. If I were seeing Nikki, I'd make fun of the humidity and her hair.

Shit.

Not thinking about her was going well so far.

> *... and if you're out driving today, try to avoid the intersection of Hope and Green near the cemetery. There was an accident last night involving three vehicles, where a blue Honda was crushed.*

Practically tripping over my feet, I fell to my knees in front of the television. Footage of a car being hauled onto the back of a tilt-tray truck filled the screen, surrounded by darkness and the street lights dappling through the rain on the camera, filmed only hours ago.

I knew that car.

No.

> *More Information about the accident has not yet been released, but we've heard one of those involved was an off-duty police officer. The intersection is closed for cleanup and will be for at least three hours while investigators assess the cause of the accident.*
>
> *Coming up—*

I didn't hear anything else.
I was already out the door.

CHAPTER
20

CADE

The automatic doors at the entrance to the hospital opened too slowly, and I shouldered my way in, drawing the attention of the nurses at the front desk.

"Kline, Nikki Kline. Where is she?"

"Are you next of kin?"

My fingers flexed at my sides as I resisted the urge to slam my palm on the desk in front of the nurse. It was only the thought of being denied the opportunity to see Nikki that was keeping me under control because I could feel my demon inside me screaming for release.

For once, it wasn't because of a desire for a fight or a fuck.

It was the protective, possessive part of me that wanted to be with my mate.

Even if she never wanted to see me again.

"I'm her... boyfriend."

The nurse studied me from under her brow, her eyes filled with sympathy as she took in my dark hair, plastered to my forehead with sweat. Nervously, I ran my hand through it, pushing it back, and held her eye contact.

"Please," I pleaded, repeating the motion. "I'm scared. I need to know she's okay."

"Of course, sweetie. Room 402. Elevator is back there."

"Do you know if..." The words were impossible to get out. The idea too much to consider, let alone speak aloud, as if I believed that by some cosmic power, saying it out loud would make it real.

Please, Nikki, no.

"I don't know the details of her condition, sir, but the doctor on duty—"

"Thanks."

The elevator would be too slow, and I bounded for the stairs, taking them three at a time and putting on a burst of supernatural speed whenever the halls were clear of witnesses. Stopping outside Nikki's door only to make a vague attempt at composing myself, I paced back and forth, shaking the tension from my hands.

The move was useless.

Pushing the door open and wincing at the squeak, a growl rumbled through my throat.

There was a man standing next to her bed.

No, not a man.

An angel.

A literal angel.

While he wasn't the first I had come across on Earth, I'd never had a proper conversation with one or anything more than a nod of recognition from me and a frown of suspicion from them.

"Who are you?" I demanded. *Why would an angel be here?*

He turned, all chiseled features and eyes bluer than blue. I ignored the look of sympathy on his face, his brows pulled together, and when he didn't answer me fast enough, a chill ran through my body, ice pulsing through my veins and freezing me to the spot.

No.

"Are you here to take her away?" My voice was gravelly with emotion I hated to admit to, and my fingers twitched with the urge to attack him, the knowledge that would be a foolish move was irrelevant when faced with the idea he was here to take Nikki away from me.

Nikki.

"I'm not here to take her away," the angel said, his voice as fucking soothing as his eyes. Shoving him to the side, I laid my eyes upon my human, my mate, my Nikki. There were no words, only a raw, guttural moan escaped my lips as I forced myself to cross the room to her. She looked so small against the hospital bed, her hair cascading around the pillow and her shoulders. She was surrounded and hooked up to tubes, IV lines, and several machines which beeped, hissed, and breathed for her.

My hands hovered above her body. I wanted to hold her hand and caress her hair, but she looked so fragile I thought I might break her if I were to touch her.

My angel.

The longer I watched, hovering helplessly over her body, the weaker I felt. My legs trembled under my own weight, and I gripped the bar on the side of her bed, the metal creaking and clanking under my weight.

It was her, she was making me weak. She *made* me weak. I thought only human blood controlled us—if a demon loves someone, because despite our reputation, we love deeply and completely, our loves become our weakness. You can create a trap using a demon's lover's blood, a circle on the ground can stop us from transforming. Here I stood next to Nikki, who had completely consumed me, who I could no longer deny my feelings for, and her being hurt was physically weakening me.

I shuddered under the weight of the knowledge that I loved her.

I *loved* her, and I had driven her to this.

She was my weakness, my love, and if she died, I

didn't want to live.

"Oh, Nikki, I'm so sorry," I whispered. When I pivoted and grabbed at the T-shirt of the angel by her bedside, he didn't flinch, but his blue eyes clouded over with the natural white of angels before he controlled his anger. "What happened to her?"

"Zaqiel," he muttered, bringing his hands to mine and removing my grip from his shirt.

"What happened to her, *Zaqiel?*"

"A car accide—"

"No fucking shit! I mean... *is she going to be okay?*" The anger exploded from me, and Zaqiel carefully arched a brow.

"If you'll calm for a moment, I will explain."

There was no calming, and I couldn't keep my eyes off Nikki, strapped to the bed so she didn't pull out her tubes and lines if she spasmed in her state. She was a prisoner of her body and this room, and I hated it.

I hated it more because it was all my fault, and I knew she'd hate it too.

Zaqiel watched me pace before sighing and leaning his shoulder against the wall. He didn't wait for me to still, observant enough to realize I wasn't going to. There was too much energy in me, and the need to protect was exercising itself with the need to bring down someone, anyone. Zaqiel was closest, but he was in no danger from me physically. An angel could take a demon any day.

"She was drunk and driving."

"She was going to the cemetery," I added. Of course, she was. With the location of the accident, there was no other explanation. Nikki was going to her father's grave as though he could offer her some peace or answers. But there'd be no peace, not after what I had put her through.

"They're still figuring out what happened, but judging by her blood alcohol level, it's likely she passed out behind the wheel. Several other cars were involved, but she was the only one hurt. Thank God."

I wheeled around, invading his space. Zaqiel was unconcerned with my show of aggression, his power vastly superior to mine. But I was fighting with pure rage and hatred and didn't doubt I could knock him down a few pegs before he ultimately bested me. "What the fuck do you mean, *thank God?*"

"No one else was hurt. Did you see the accident? No," he added firmly before I could answer, "Well, I did. We're lucky no one died."

"*Look at her!*"

"If it weren't for me, she *would* be dead, and I'd appreciate it if you stopped treating me like the enemy, demon."

Through gritted teeth, I muttered, "Cade," as I stepped away from Zaqiel.

He waited for me to interrupt again, and when I didn't, he continued, "She was choking on her own vomit. I cleared her airway and removed her from the vehicle while keeping her neck and spine straight. I told the other drivers to stay away, so I could destroy the car as I needed to get her legs out so she wasn't trapped, and we didn't have to wait for the paramedics. I stayed with her until the ambulance came."

I wanted to thank him, but I couldn't find the words. "Is she going to die?"

The pause before he answered only increased the black hole that had been living inside my chest. God, I was a horrible being. If I weren't already from Hell, I would be going straight there. I'd end my own life right now if it meant I'd spent an eternity being tortured for what I had done. I deserved nothing less. But there was no afterlife for exiled demons.

Zaqiel cleared his throat. This was the first show of emotion I had seen from the otherwise stoic angel, and I wasn't sure if that helped or made me feel worse. "She has a cerebral contusion and a small hemorrhage."

"Z-Zaqiel," my voice was as broken as my heart. "Tell me what that *means.*"

"It means, Cade, that her brain is swelling and pushing against her skull. This damages the part of the brain, the reticular activating system, that controls arousal from sleep." He looked at Nikki, watching the machines beep and utter their soothing sounds of breathing life for a moment. "She's in a coma, and all we can do is wait until she wakes."

Getting out the words was hard, pushing them through my chest and out my throat, cutting daggers into me as they came. All I could think about was Nikki trapped in eternal sleep. Was she dreaming? What if she was having nightmares? "And if..." I closed my eyes, *no, no if*, "... *when* she wakes?"

"She'll need physical therapy to walk and talk properly again. She may suffer minor memory lapses for a few months. But..." he dragged his fingers through her hair, and I wanted to rip his arm off, only allowing the move because he saved her life. "*When* she wakes, she'll be okay. She's strong, I can tell."

"You have no idea," I choked out.

Collapsing in the only available chair in the room, I pulled it up next to her bed, shuffled my feet across the floor, and rested my head in my hands. I groaned loudly before looking up and taking Nikki's hand, carefully avoiding the IV line and stroking her wrist.

"You love her, don't you?" Zaqiel asked.

"Yes." There was no point in lying.

"Does she know what you are?"

"Yes." I was quieter this time.

Zaqiel didn't ask how she had reacted. I suspect he didn't need to. Her reaction was staring him in the face, lying in a hospital bed after an accident that almost took her life were it not for the intervention of an angel. He grabbed his jacket from the end of Nikki's bed and shrugged it on. "I'll come back and check on her in a few days."

"I'll be here."

The sympathetic pull of his brow definitely made it worse. "I know. I'll tell the doctors you're staying." I doubted visitors were allowed to hang around every hour of the day, but there was no way in hell I was leaving anyway, and Zaqiel must have known that. Perhaps he had a rapport with the doctors here. I didn't particularly care. If I was questioned, I'd fight to stay.

Let them try and stop me.

Zaqiel was just about at the door when I found the words. "How can I ever repay you for saving my heart?"

He paused, his back to me. "You don't need to. I'm an angel. I go where I'm needed."

"And I'm a demon..." he turned then, his eyes blazing white meeting my yellow, "... and we don't take these things lightly. You saved my love, my life, and I owe you mine."

Zaqiel almost smiled, a slight lifting of his lip before it disappeared. "You're all God's children, and I am his vessel."

I nodded. I didn't know what else to say. Demons as God's children seemed obscene, but it made sense, and while most of us would deny it until our last breath left us, I guess it had to be true. The legends of the Devil being a fallen angel, cast down to the underworld and running a world of demons and darkness, while never proven, was still the most accepted tale. I stayed silent as I watched him leave, wondering if he knew the answers. But watching Nikki, I didn't care. I left that world behind before I met her, and then when I had her, I was certain I'd never need to return.

Nikki's eyes were moving behind her closed lids, and I reached out and stroked her forehead, telling her I was there, that I loved her, and that I was sorry. The movement eased, and I hoped she could hear and forgive me. I hoped she was having nice dreams if she were dreaming at all, that she was in no pain, and her heart didn't ache like mine. I'd bear the pain for her a thousand times over and would have my kin dig into my chest and remove my mark, a torment I'd live through again and again if I could take away the pain I had caused Nikki.

And Zaqiel, I'd give him my life if I had to for saving mine.

CHAPTER
21

NIKKI

This wasn't my bed.

There was no denying I had drunk too much, *way* too much, but my memories should be clearer.

I was on my way to the cemetery to visit my father's grave, the man who was now nothing more than a stranger to me, information I had found with the cost of my sanity. Beyond that, the memories were nothing but confusion. There was screaming. Was it the car tires or was it coming from me, I couldn't be sure. At the same time, there was pain and darkness, and since then, more confusion. Bright lights and sounds I couldn't decipher or understand. They could have been voices, music, or the grinding of machines, I wouldn't have been able to say with any certainty.

Now, the darkness remained, but a pulsing pain

in my head was making itself known. I tried to lift my hand to rub my forehead. I couldn't. Was I being restrained or was I paralyzed? There were so many things I didn't know, and I groaned, the sound tearing through my throat, dry and uncomfortable.

"Shh… it's okay."

The voice was deep, soothing, and accompanied by a sweep of cool fingers across my forehead.

Cade?

I wanted to reach out to him or say his name. I felt my lips part, dry and parched, and my tongue move in my mouth, but the sound didn't come. Did I want Cade to be here with me? Wherever *here* was, I wasn't sure. The lights were bright and painful, so I kept my eyes closed, though I'm not sure if I could open them if I wanted to. I remembered Cade as I knew him. I remembered him being there when I needed him more than once and the feel of his hands on my body.

Moaning, I also remembered when he changed into a monster, and my life spiraled out of control more than it already had. But somehow, that didn't matter so much because the comfort of his presence surrounded me. Cade had never once tried to hurt me. In fact, he'd protected me.

"Ca…" I managed the first part of his name and nothing more. Choking back a dry sob, the hand was on my face again, stroking my cheek. *Why was it so hard to talk?*

"No, I'm a friend. Keep still. You've been in an accident."

Pulling my eyes open, I blinked against the bright light above my head. Turning my gaze, my eyes fell upon a man standing next to my bed.

He was beautiful.

There was no other way to describe him. All chiseled features with blue eyes and brown hair kept cut close to his scalp. He was stroking my face, and there was something about simply looking at him that was soothing. He looked like an angel.

"I'm dead?" I whispered.

His lip twitched, almost a smile. "No, you're okay. You were in an accident, but you are fine. He never left your side."

"What?"

The man nodded to my other side. "Cade, he's been here by your side every minute."

The tears that prickled were painful. Everything was painful. My throat was dry and raw, my head throbbing, but I managed to roll slightly to the other side and stare blearily at Cade asleep in the chair next to my bed. He looked like hell, and I realized the irony of thinking that considering I was the one in the hospital bed, judging by the tubes and lines surrounding me. I couldn't feel them, but they were there, making me feel like a science experiment. I never was good with being at the doctor's office.

Cade. He had overgrown stubble I'd never seen

him with before, black circles under his eyes, and his hair was oily and needed a wash.

"He's a good man," the man said, touching my cheek and turning my gaze back to him.

I wanted to shake my head but only managed a frown. "Noo… not man."

"Nikki, please listen to me. Whatever you've seen, I promise you that's not all there is to him. Every being has an aura, and while his DNA may be demon, he's too good to be truly considered one. He loves you."

"Not… Devil?"

"He's not Satan. He's a demon."

Unable to bring myself to nod, I simply pulled my gaze from his face and stared out of focus at his chest. Good to know I didn't have sex with the Devil himself. Although, a demon wasn't much better. Too much information was given to me at once, and I struggled to process it, to put the words together into sentences and pull them through my mind in an order that made sense. I took a couple of minutes to let the words come to me, to let them swirl around in my aching head until I could bring them to some semblance of sense.

He *loves* me?

I tried to shake my head again. I needed to make this man understand. "I saw… you haven't seen… what I saw."

"You'd be surprised what I've seen."

When I looked at him again, his eyes were white, a cloudy covering over the blue that swirled for a moment before dissipating. I yanked against the restraints on my hands, jolting them against the metal bars of the bed, and he shushed me again, smoothing my hair from my face.

"There is much to this world you know not of." The tears were coming again as I listened to him speak, and when I pulled my gaze back to his face, his eyes were that perfect ocean blue again. "All you need to know is this… he loves you, and you'll never, *never* be unsafe with him." He wiped away the tears from my cheeks with his thumbs. "Sleep now. I'll tell him you're okay, I promise."

"Who… you?" My eyes were already closing, and the feel of his touch was soothing, calming my nerves and pain.

"You already know, but I don't matter. Just let yourself love him back."

Do I already know? His words confused me, so little made sense right now. I clung to the things he said and kept them locked in my mind, hoping they would make sense when I woke next, but right now, I was tired. I wanted to watch Cade sleep, to see him as a man, as a human, and remind myself I wasn't crazy for feeling how I did. For having my heart skip a beat every time I saw him leaning in the doorway with the beat-up leather jacket and his hair falling in front of his brows.

What did I know of angels and demons? Only the common lore.

I never considered myself religious, except toward the end of my mother's life when I prayed for her health, and if that couldn't be provided, I prayed that she'd be safe, happy, and without pain wherever she was going. Maybe I should have prayed for the strength to live without her, for that was the hardest thing to learn, only made bearable by my father's support. Was his love a lie? Or just his life? How could a man treat me the way he did, be the father he was, when behind closed doors, he was a murderer worthy of eternity in Hell?

I loved Cade, I did, but I didn't want to.

Especially now that I knew what he was.

Did that make me a bad person?

I managed to pull myself to move enough to roll my head and watch Cade, he looked troubled in his sleep, and I wanted to tell him I was okay. God, what was wrong with me? He was a demon and didn't need comforting. But there was something so soothing about the man's words, he could have told me anything, and I'd have believed him. His touch felt like he was pushing all the stress and pain from my body, and I was left relaxed.

It was near impossible to correlate the Cade before me now with the monster I had seen in my home, even as my vision grew fuzzy and my eyelids began to droop. Should I try harder to remind myself they were one and the same? If my father had taught me anything, it was even the darkest men were capable of love.

Probably not a great lesson to learn, but while everything was falling apart around me, every truth I thought I knew and held close, Cade was this passionate being who made me feel more alive than I had in years.

Let yourself love him back.

Yes.

Yes, angel man, I think I will.

CHAPTER 22

CADE

Zaqiel told me she woke after nine days, and it was during one of the rare times I was asleep. As a demon, I could comfortably go without sleep for a couple of days, and at a push, I could make it to almost a week, which is exactly what I'd done. But in the end, emotional and physical exhaustion had won out, and I was forced to fall back in the uncomfortable chair and allow my body the sleep it craved. I'd been out for seven hours, and during that time, Zaqiel had come back to visit Nikki again, and she had regained consciousness for a few minutes.

He wasn't pleased with the way I grabbed at his shirt and shook him, demanding to know what she said and what he said back, but it seemed he had accepted this as how we communicated now and no longer insisted I let him go before he'd answer my questions. Somehow, his patience only increased my anger. The doctor I had hassled—once I got the information from Zaqiel—told me Nikki's waking was an excellent sign, given how lucid Zaqiel had advised she was, but she'd still need more rest.

She could wake again at any time, though, and I'd be there.

When the room was clear of doctors, the angel told me Nikki remembered my transformation into my demon form and was still frightened, but when she had woken, she had tried to call for me. He said he could see it in her eyes, the mixture of fear, pain, and confusion.

He said he'd told her I loved her, and I wished he hadn't. I didn't want to burden her with that fact. If she wanted to walk away from me after what she had witnessed, I wouldn't stop her, and I didn't want her to feel any guilt over that.

All the guilt was mine to bear.

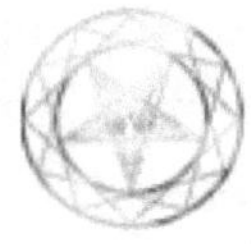

Thirty-six hours later, Nikki stirred again.

I almost tripped over the leg of the chair in my rush to be by her side, forgetting for a moment that my presence may frighten her. I held onto the line of hope Zaqiel had thrown me, that she wanted me when she woke up last time. I could only hope it was from some deep part of her that loved me back and not through confusion or some side effect of the accident.

She moaned softly, her eyelids fluttering. The restraints had been removed from her hands. The doctors felt the chances of her yanking out the lines were unlikely at this stage, and I was thankful she didn't have to wake trapped and afraid again. They had removed the feeding tube around six hours ago, hoping this would assist in waking on her own.

"Nikki, it's okay, angel. I'm here."

Would my presence be a comfort or only make her fear worse?

"Demon," she pushed the word out, and my spine stiffened as I prepared myself for the blow that she didn't want me here, she didn't love or need me as I did her, and she wanted me to leave. Gritting my teeth against tears that I absolutely wasn't going to allow to fall, I grabbed the plastic cup of water off the side table and offered her the straw. Her lips fumbled around it before she took a few grateful sips of the cool liquid, her eyes never leaving mine.

"Do you want me to leave?" I asked quietly, placing the cup back on the table.

Nikki frowned. "I didn't fuck the Devil."

My eyebrows shot up. Is that what she thought?

That I was the Devil himself? Granted, being a demon wasn't likely to be any better to a frightened human, but Zaqiel hadn't told me he'd made the clarification with her. "No," I muttered, brushing a thumb across her forehead to ease her frown, "I'm not the Devil. I'm a demon, but I don't want to be, not really."

She simply blinked at me, a look of innocence and curiosity on her face. I didn't know exactly what to say but felt I should keep talking to her. "I never quite fit in at home... in Hell. That's why I came to Earth. But I never thought I'd find someone like you, and I never thought myself capable of love." Her eyes widened, and her fingers gripped the sheet, albeit weakly, but she said nothing, so I continued, "I'll understand if you never want to see me again, and I know words can't take it back, but I'm sorry for what you witnessed. But if you're not frightened of me, I hope you can remember who I was before you saw the transformation because that's the *real* me. I'll spend the rest of my life making it up to you and showing you you're safe and loved if you'll have me."

"Love me?"

She was still in so much pain. I could see it in the way her throat worked around the words and the grimace when she swallowed painfully after asking. Nikki was choosing her words carefully, but I didn't doubt there'd be a world of questions later. It broke something in me to know that her first question was asking if I loved her.

"Yes," I whispered, holding her eye contact. "I love you."

"Time." She sighed.

I understood it would take her time. "As much as you need."

Her eyes shimmered with emotion, and I kissed her forehead. "I'm going to get the doctor."

As the days went on, Nikki became more lucid and capable, and I still hadn't left the hospital. Smithy knew where I was and hadn't called me since I contacted him two days after the accident. At least knowing enough about me to know if pushed, I'd throw the job in, and also that I would call him when I was ready to and not a minute earlier. When Nikki mumbled a complaint about missing home cooking, she didn't want me to speak to the nurses because she understood the work that went into hospital food. I tried it, it wasn't bad at all, but I knew what she meant.

Besides, the woman could cook, and I missed it too.

Slipping out of her room when the nurse came in to bathe her and begin explaining the physical therapy, I returned with a quiche from the canteen on the ground floor. Nikki's eyes followed my movement into the room, that frown on her brow becoming a familiar part of her as she worked her way through each day. Then her eyes widened with recognition when she realized what I was attempting to replicate with her, and she laughed quietly, patting the side of her bed.

It was the first invitation I'd had to get closer to her, so while I took it, I did so tentatively, trying not to think about what other demons would think of me. All emotions, empathy, and compassion, all this bullshit we didn't normally deal with, not to mention the fucking quiche. But I stopped caring what they thought the moment they shredded my mark from my chest.

Except Frank, and while I'd never admit it to him, I cared what he thought.

I should really call him.

Sliding the quiche onto her tray, I offered, "Do you want to eat?"

She smiled, and my chest swelled. She was getting color back into her face, sitting up no longer taking all the energy from her. Though she did grow tired quickly, she wouldn't admit it and only relaxed when I'd put on the television and sat in silence until she settled into her pillows. Nikki's eyes were bright as they watched mine, and her lips curved into a slight smile that reminded me of what I was fighting for.

Behind the smile, was she thinking of me in my true form?

"Soon," she said, patting my hand before drawing away. "Quiche is just as good cold."

I scrunched up my nose. "If you say so."

"Let's talk."

"Okay."

We both waited in silence, and I shifted uncomfortably. Was she waiting for me to make the first move to begin this conversation? I didn't know where to begin. "Do you remember…"

"Yes," she cut me off, averting her eyes from mine. "Yes, I remember… the night before the accident."

In the silence that followed, the cavern opened up in my chest again. While waiting for her to become more coherent and comfortable, the words hung unspoken between us. When she couldn't speak enough to hold a conversation, her eyes would watch me, study me, while I kept up small talk that made me as uncomfortable as it did her. But she never asked me to leave or indicated that she wanted me to. Nikki never screamed, cried, or looked terrified when I was near, and I supposed I should be thankful for at least that.

"It's hard," she mumbled finally.

"I know."

After flitting her gaze around the room, she finally settled on my eyes again, and all the confusion I saw there, I wanted to be able to make disappear. "Has anyone else ever seen..." she trailed off.

"Any other human?" She nodded, her jaw tensing, and my hand twitched. I wanted to hold her hand while we talked, but would that be too much for her? I wasn't used to treading carefully. We had been so good together, physically and otherwise, and so comfortable, but now I was second-guessing every move I made. "No, you're the only one." When she looked away again, I added, "But it was an accident, Nikki. I never wanted you to see that part of me."

"Were you ever going to tell me?"

Fuck. "Eventually." The purse of her lips told me she wasn't happy with that answer. "You have to understand it's not easy to bring up. Would you have believed me if I outright told you?"

"I might have."

"Nikki, there's no way. Not with everything else going on. I wanted to help solve your father's murder so you could move on with your life. Regardless of if I felt he deserved your loyalty. I wanted that *for you.*"

"Help solve?" She paused, frowning again. It seemed almost a permanent fixture now. "Did the clue in my mailbox come from you?"

"Yes."

The frown deepened again as she worked through her thoughts. Nikki wasn't stupid. I couldn't have gone to her and simply told her to check out the club because why should she believe me? And that would only lead to awkward questions.

Dammit.

"Nikki, look..." She dragged her gaze back to mine as I sighed. "I didn't go about things the right way, I know that. I've made so many mistakes when it came to you and how I dealt with things. But everything I did, I did because I thought it was the right thing, and I only wanted to help and protect you."

"Why?"

Why was a very good question. "Because I've never felt more human than when I'm with you. I like who I am with you." I grimaced, the display of emotion felt strange when spoken aloud, strange and foolish.

Her expression softened, and my hand twitched again. This time she noticed the movement and slid her fingers along the cotton bedsheets before intertwining them with mine. "I had dreams, you know?" I said nothing and waited for her to continue, squeezing her hand. "Like I was in my everyday life, but it was... *off.* Every now and then, you would come to me and tell me everything was going to be okay, and I'd ask you *why are you telling me this?* I couldn't understand why you'd be reassuring me over nothing. Sometimes they were nightmares, and I was being chased or hunted. And in those dreams, you were there, as a demon…" She paused as I flinched and squeezed my eyes shut because I didn't want to be haunting her dreams. "No, no, Cade, listen…"

I looked at her beautiful hazel eyes, her white-blonde hair falling around her shoulders, and her lips slightly parted. I wanted to kiss her.

"You were the demon, but you weren't the one chasing me. You were the one *saving* me." She sighed, and I could see the conflict fighting within her eyes. "I guess you were just doing your job… with Dad, I mean… your fucked-up demon job."

"I'm sorry."

What else could I say? Fuck, emotions were so complicated. Sex and fighting were fun and easy, but this? This connection with another being, this wanting to keep them safe above all else thing? It made me stupid. I'd made some fucking idiotic decisions since I met Nikki, and while I'd do some things differently, I wouldn't take it back. I'd run through metaphorical and physical hell over and over again if it gave her peace.

"Humans can be so fucked up," she whispered and shook her head slightly. She looked at our intertwined hands while her fingers played with mine as she traced the lines on my palm. I was as mesmerized by the movement as she was because her touch was pure, and I wanted more.

"Everything I thought I knew about my family was a lie, and when I tried to do the right thing, I was blocked by corruption and crooks. People who didn't play by the rules were impossible to get around because I wanted to keep to my morals. People, Cade, people fucked me over. But you…" There were tears in her eyes, and her lips lifted into a small smile for a beat when I wiped one away as it ran down her freckled cheek. "You only ever looked out for me, cared for me. You did some *stupid fucking shit…*" her lip twitched, it was almost a smile, "… but it was *for me.*"

I didn't know what to say.

"Who would have thought…" Nikki sighed, tilted her head, and closed her eyes as she leaned into my palm, "… a demon would be my savior among humans?"

CHAPTER 23

NIKKI

Physical therapy was a drag, and it was frustrating as hell. I *knew* how to walk, I *knew* how to pick up a cup and drink, so why wouldn't my fucking body cooperate with me? I'd be thinking something, demanding my subconscious mind relay the message to my legs, but it simply didn't happen like that. Not straight away, anyway.

The nurses said they were happy with my progress, but I demanded faster. I wanted my reflexes back. I wanted to be able to fight, to look after myself, to shoot with accuracy, and drive like I was in the fucking Formula One.

Time, they kept telling me. *It will take time.*

Fucking hell.

Cade was there all day and every day until sometimes I'd kick him out and demand he go have a shower, get something to eat, and maybe grab a couple of hours of decent sleep. He fucking *snarled* at me at one point when I became too insistent and told him he stunk and needed a shower.

"How do I respond to that demon shit?" I asked. "Smack you on the nose with a rolled-up newspaper?"

His curled lip turned into a smirk, but the rumble in his chest increased until it was an animalistic growl, somehow sexier, knowing that beneath his skin, he wasn't human.

How messed up am I?

"No," he growled out, placing his palms on the pillows on either side of my head and leaning in close, his lips hovering over mine as I pouted slightly, desperate for contact he was denying me. He wouldn't touch me more than a peck on the cheek and a handhold while I was recovering, and it was a matter of the mind being willing but the flesh being weak. But *damn,* when he teased me like this, it drove me crazy. "But maybe I could smack you on the ass a few times until you learn to speak to me with some respect."

"Would that make you happy, *sir?*"

He groaned and brushed his lips against mine. "You are in so much trouble when you're better."

"Can't I be in trouble now?"

"*Fuck,* Nikki, you're killing me."

He glanced around, tilting back to make sure the

hallway was clear before he returned to his position, leaning over me and dominating the space around me. He gently traced his fingers down my cheek and neck, then further down, brushing against my breasts through my hospital gown. I gasped, and his eyes shot to mine, the lust broken by concern. I think he expected me to still be afraid of him, at least in part, and while I'd admitted to him I wasn't keen to see his demon form again any time soon, I hadn't been able to look at him as anything other than the Cade I knew, and that was more than enough for now.

Because the most stable part of my life was a fucking demon.

Torturously slow, he dragged his palm down my body before finally sliding under the sheets at my hips and hitching up my gown, tracing teasing patterns along the fabric of my underwear. When I gasped his name, he pressed his lips to mine, a chaste kiss as he shifted my panties to the side and ran his fingers between my pussy lips, already wet for him.

Cade growled again, and when I sighed as he pushed a finger into me, he clasped his other hand over my mouth. "Shh, angel. Keep quiet."

He pinned me with his gaze, his forehead resting against mine as he pumped his finger in and out of me before adding another one. I opened my legs to accommodate his touch, bucking my hips against him and desperate for more until his thumb found my clit. I moaned against his hand, and his eyes flashed yellow, making me gasp. He had explained to me his nature and that he needed release to keep his demon under control. Circumstances had taught him more control than he had thought himself capable of, but I loved that the feeling of me clenching around his fingers as he beckoned me to my peak was enough to make his control slip, even just a little.

My breathing became ragged as he whispered, "Are you going to come for me?"

I nodded against his hand, and he growled again until he needed to press on my mouth so hard to silence me, I fell back against the pillows as I cried out against his palm, coming around his fingers as my orgasm shook me and made my leg tremble with the release.

An insistent beeping sound broke the moment, and a nurse rushed into the room, straightening a bobby pin in her hair as Cade hastily removed his hand from under the sheets. Without a word, the nurse grabbed my wrist, feeling my pulse while pressing buttons on one of the machines that monitored me. Slowly, her eyes came to mine, taking in my flushed cheeks and disheveled hair before her gaze settled on Cade with that smug fucking grin plastered on his face.

"She needs to rest," the nurse berated, looking at

Cade over her glasses as though he were an insolent child. I'd had enough of resting, but I wasn't about to argue with the stern woman as she turned her accusing glare to me. I turned my lips down forcefully to hide the smirk that threatened to surface as Cade made obscene gestures with his tongue behind the nurse's back.

"Go home," she said to Cade, and with another visual sweep over him, added, "… and take a shower."

He nodded, shoving his hands in his pockets after blowing me a kiss, winking at me before he left, and leaving me wanting more.

Niles came to visit later that day, the only one from the precinct who had, which wasn't entirely surprising. I hadn't worked particularly hard, if at all, at making friends there. It was probably something I'd need to rectify, maybe even request a transfer and start afresh right after I caught up and made things right with my existing friends for my extended absence. The precinct had sent me a humongous bunch of flowers, though. However, I wondered if that was only Niles' doing as well.

Flowers weren't normally my thing, but I'll admit the sunflowers brightened up the otherwise drab room, and since I was going to be here for a while, I'd take any comfort I could get.

I wouldn't be able to return to work straightaway, even after I was fully recovered. I'd been suspended for three months, and the three months started after my discharge from the hospital. The force doesn't look too kindly upon drunk driving. I guess they have to maintain some illusion of integrity.

"Kline," Niles said, pulling up the empty chair next to my bed.

"Hey, Lute."

His stoic expression wavered for a moment as he looked at me, sweeping his gaze over the machines and lines before coming back to my eyes. "What happened?"

"I'm sure you already know."

"Maybe, but I want to hear it from you."

Sighing, I slid down on my pillows, taking a moment to curl and stretch my toes under the sheets. With the physical therapy, I liked the reminder that I was ultimately still in control of my body, even if it wasn't cooperating all the time. "I was stupid… I drove while incredibly fucking drunk and crashed my car. I'm lucky I didn't kill anyone or myself."

"I know that much. What I want to know is *why?*"

I searched his eyes, and when he went to take my hand, I slid it away. "Because I had just found out that my father and Murphy were the same person."

Niles's denial was immediate. "Nikki, no, that's not possible."

"Isn't it? He was incredibly good at what he did, Niles. How do you know he didn't have an entirely secret life under another name? Or several lives."

"Can you prove this at all?"

The image of Cade in his demon form flooded my mind. It was hard to argue when faced with the reality of an afterlife, and then a demon was telling you your father was in Hell and why. I had drilled Cade with all these questions already, although sometimes he had to repeat some things over the days. I now knew as much about my father's underground operation as Cade did, and he was absolutely certain of his identity because when he had asked him about me, Mitch Murphy... Garrett Porter... my dad had reacted to the mention of me.

"Not exactly," I muttered, looking away as his face fell with sympathy. "But just take my word for it, okay? It's been proven to me, but unfortunately, I can't prove it to anyone else..." hitting him with a hard stare before looking away again, I stared out the window, "... yet."

But proving it to others wasn't important because this went too deep. The complications had only increased when Emrick had taken over the business and assets but left my father alive. Then there was Rueben Cole, the man I suspected was the asshole who had threatened me and was responsible for the deaths of Torres and Kim as well as my father. He was cleaning house, tying up loose ends, but for what purpose? If there were two opposing crime syndicates, Emrick and Cole, both with their hands in the police force, how deep did this go? Were they in politics as well? Did they have the mayor under their thumbs? With cash to throw around, it wouldn't surprise me.

So, proving my father's identity wasn't the issue, but I was still determined to find the man responsible for his death and bring him to justice. Despite what Cade may feel, I wanted to avenge his murder. He was a lot of things, but he was still my family.

However, I was going to take a few steps back because given the kind of man he was, Murphy didn't deserve my full attention and time. He could have some of me but not all. I had a life to live, and I wanted to get back to work, be with Cade, reconnect with my friends, and start to feel human again.

"Can I ask you a question, off the record?" I asked. Niles watched me for a moment. I'm certain he knew where this was going, but he nodded. "Were you instructed not to look into my father's death? And if so, do you know by who?"

Niles drummed his fingers on my bed, the soft padding sound on the sheets joining with the beeps of the machines around me while he considered his words. "The case was handled by detectives who had been in the force for many years. When they made their call, no one questioned it." I nodded, and Niles added, "Whatever is going on, Nikki, I'm not a part of it."

I eyed him. "Not directly, no, but the entire force is under the control of those who run the crime around here."

He didn't argue because he already knew.

"And Officers Kim and Torres?" I pushed. If they were killed because Cole was *cleaning house*, they may have been weak links, young and inexperienced, maybe newly inducted into the corrupt bullshit they'd been lured into. What's the saying? *Last hired, first fired.*

"Same deal. The cases were closed. No one asked questions... no one ever does." Niles almost smirked, his eyes sparkling. "Except you."

"Yeah, and look where that got me."

Closing my eyes, I was suddenly tired. This went too deep, and even if I were to find Cole and kill him, another one would simply pop up in his place. Cade had warned me to stay the fuck away from Emrick, and I'm certain there was something he wasn't telling me. Was Emrick a demon as well? Wouldn't that be fucking something? A fucking crime boss who wasn't even human. We'd all be in serious trouble then.

So, if I couldn't do anything to change the situation, what could I do?

I had no doubt I'd go back to being a cop. When the doctors were satisfied I was physically okay, and once I'd completed the mandatory leave for recovery to monitor my condition and make sure the memory lapses were getting better and not worse, *and* once I completed my suspension, I would go back. I couldn't solve all the problems, but there were still many good people in this city who needed help and protection. They needed people on the police force who were there for *them.*

On the side, I'd track down this Cole guy and see what I could find out about him. Eventually, he'd answer for the death of my father.

Other injustices I saw, I wasn't sure I'd be able to keep my mouth shut about. But it would be a balancing game because if I wanted to remain on the force to do what good work I could, I'd have to keep my head down. But now I had Cade on my side, we'd find a way to help those that needed it, even if it meant skirting the system somewhat. The lines of black and white had well and truly been blurred into worlds of gray, and now that my eyes were open to everything that was going on, I needed to work smart and not put so much blind faith in a system that was as corruptible as the people who worked for it.

Niles patted my hand, and I let him, opening one eye and watching as he stood. "You need to rest. I'll come visit you again soon."

Nodding, I allowed myself to fall back into the pillows and my thoughts, and eventually, my dreams were of a corrupt world and all the monsters that lived inside the people within the city.

And a demon, who saved me.

CHAPTER
24

CADE

While Nikki was in therapy one day, I took the time to wander outside the hospital, taking a moment to lean my back against the warm bricks and close my eyes, absorbing the glow of the midday sun. I was happy to stay inside, but Nikki didn't like witnesses to her rehabilitation. She hated the way her forehead sweat and her cheeks flushed when she did her exercises and how she'd slip midstep on occasion. There was no room for error in her mind, and while I offered to help, maybe lie back with my cock exposed to give her something to run toward, she laughed before turning serious and told me to go for a walk.

A nice relaxing walk, not exactly something demons were known for enjoying.

Rolling my eyes, I pushed myself from the wall

and jammed my hands in my pockets before continuing around the perimeter of the building, not wanting to stray too far.

I hadn't been back to work since Nikki's accident and consequently had no money, a result of which was being evicted from my apartment. I didn't care much. I had little to nothing in there besides the ratty furniture the place came with. Since then, Nikki had given me keys to her place to take a shower, get some sleep outside of the hospital, and bring her food—she favored fresh avocados, fuck knows why—and it seemed to be an unspoken thing I'd be moving in with her when she was discharged. After asking if she wanted me to tidy up her place, she'd laughed, then I'd laughed, and we both realized it was never going to happen.

The skin on the back of my neck prickled a split second before a hand was slapped over my mouth, and I was dragged backward into a dark crevice that was a fire escape. While I could have stopped them from taking me, my lips curled into a smirk behind their hand, and I thought it would be more fun to allow myself to be taken, and then let out the part of my demon desperate for a fight at the last second.

The sting of the knife as it was pressed against the back of my throat told me this wasn't the situation I thought it was.

Silver.

Silver didn't kill demons, but it hurt like hell and would take longer to heal. This told me several important details. Firstly, this wasn't a random attack. Secondly, my attacker *knew* I was a demon, and third, I guess they knew enough to know if they pushed the blade through my throat and were able to restrain me so I couldn't remove it, I'd choke on my own blood. I couldn't heal around silver, I'd have to get the blade out, and if I couldn't, I'd die.

After that, they would remove my heart and burn it, and that would be that.

So, I stilled.

"I'm going to remove my hand. I'm not here to kill you. I don't need any more enemies than I already have, and..." the deep voice chuckled next to my neck as the silver knife twisted slightly, stinging against my skin. "I think Nikki hates me enough already for killing her father, so I wouldn't want to take her boyfriend too."

"Who are you?" The words were out the second he removed his hand, and he responded only by pushing the blade harder against my neck, definitely drawing blood.

"I only want to talk."

"Why?"

"I've cleaned up, and I'm ready to clear out of this city. Emrick's empire is growing too quickly, and this fucking hole of a city isn't worth the effort to keep. I have roots elsewhere, and I'm moving on."

"Cole," I muttered, attempting to turn my head and having a hand grab my chin and cheek, forcing me to look forward again. He wore some kind of jewelry on his hand, a metal ring on his middle finger with a chain that linked to a claw-like attachment that dug into my skin and seared. Silver again. There was silence when I had spoken his name, and no response was the same as acknowledgment. He didn't ask how I knew his name, and I suppose it didn't make much difference to him. "What's this got to do with me?"

"Tell sweet Nicola to let the past go. I don't want any bullshit from this place following me to my new home, but someone I respect has told me she's not to be killed. Otherwise, I'd have gutted her already."

A low growl rumbled through my throat, and he responded only with a chuckle. I wanted to turn and rip him to shreds, but Nikki would want me to get information. We'd discussed this, her plans moving forward. Besides, killing a human with intent would have me banished from Earth, and since I was already banished from Hell, that would mean my death.

"You're human," I finally said.

"Yes, but you're not, *demon.*"

"How do you know that?"

"One doesn't get to be in this business in this city for as long as I have without learning a thing or two about the players. And let me tell you, there are plenty of your lot running around up here, especially in my line of work. You can be quite useful, pure strength-for-hire. You, however, seem to have morals for some reason, though… strange."

"We're not here to talk about me."

"You're right, we're talking about your girlfriend. Tell her to back the fuck off, for if she comes for me, I'll be ready, and any loyalty I hold to those who asked me not to kill her will become moot. I'll kill her in front of you, slowly, painfully, making you take in every scream and tear, and then I'll kill you."

I was beginning to tremble, my demon screaming to get out, every protective nerve in my body shrieking to be let loose and kill this fucking guy. But I had to think of Nikki. I couldn't help her if I were dead, whether by Rueben Cole's hand or by punishment. My muscles rippled with the effort of keeping my demon inside, and I doubted I'd have the self-control not to kill him if I started an attack.

"Who's protecting her?" A thought struck me, and I went with it. "Is it her brother?"

Another chuckle, and I wondered if I could rip his face off without killing him. Some sort of fucked-up loophole where I get to take my rage out on this asshole without being banished from Earth. "He had plans for our sweet little Nicola, long-term plans, and one day he'll come for her."

"Where is he?"

"No level of demonic tone in your voice will make

me answer that question, Cade. I know where my loyalties, as flimsy as they may be, lie."

"Where are you going?"

"Away. Don't try to find me. Pass on the message." Cole slashed at the back of my throat with the silver knife, and the stinging pain radiated through my body. In the moment of weakness, he grabbed the side of my face, slamming my head into the wall. As he moved to leave, I reached out and snatched at his jacket, and he turned, a black scarf covering the lower half of his face. His eyes, green and vibrant, blazed with fury as he clawed at me with the silver claw on his middle finger, leaving a slice down my cheek. "Stop. If I don't get back, my men have instructions to come for Nicola, and you won't be able to protect her from all of them."

Grinding my teeth, I froze on the spot, glaring at him and imprinting those eyes in my mind forever. Next time I saw those eyes, I'd find a way to take him down without losing Nikki. I couldn't know for sure if he was telling the truth, but I couldn't risk it.

We both knew how deep this ran.

Were there hospital workers in on it?

Were there nurses under Cole's payroll, primed and ready to kill Nikki in her sleep if he asked?

His eyes crinkled as he smiled before turning and walking away.

With eight weeks of physical and speech therapy, Nikki was ready to kick a hole through the wall if one more person asked her to stretch her legs using a resistance band. She hadn't had a memory lapse in over a week and rarely tripped over words or sentences now, although sometimes she still got confused, misunderstanding a word or unable to find a word she wanted. Nikki found this more frustrating than anything, and all the reassurance she'd eventually be back to normal wasn't enough for her. She was stubborn and wanted results *now*. Having been assigned a further eight weeks off with checkups on her progress every two weeks, then she should be able to officially be signed off to be fit for work.

Then start her suspension.

Nikki had thrown the sheets to the side when I told her about the interaction with Cole, asking me why I didn't do a citizen's arrest or some bullshit. I explained his threat to her life and she told me she wasn't afraid. I'd grabbed her face, making her look into my eyes and hoping she could see the fear that hid in them. Because I *was* afraid of losing her, and the memory of the feelings that tore my body apart when I'd seen her in the hospital bed that first time stayed with me, reminding me how fragile she was.

Normally, I'm certain she'd complain about being forced to take time off work, but the way she backed me against the wall in the elevator as we left the hospital, grabbing my cock through my pants and whispering naughty desires against my ear, I'm sure we'd find plenty of ways to pass the time. I wanted to take her straight back to her place to play out these desires, but there was one stop Nikki insisted on making first.

Emrick's.

I wasn't thrilled about it, but I understood. She was taking a step in a better direction, but first, she had some loose ends to tie off. Since Nikki's car had been a write-off, something she was incredibly upset about, I picked her up from the hospital in a cheap run-around I'd bought in exchange for a handful of moving jobs. The car idled so rough at traffic lights that it felt like it would die any second, but it took us to Emrick's club. We were allowed in without issue, although, of course, we were patted down before being permitted to go upstairs.

Emrick sat in the same chair, glancing over the balcony at the small crowd milling around—an afternoon crowd getting in a few drinks before the place became packed. He didn't stir when we came in, and we waited for a beat by the door for him to say or do anything that indicated he was aware of our presence. The first sign was a smirk creeping along his face, only partially visible through his fingers as he rested his chin on his palm.

"Good to see you two love birds are still together," he purred out.

"No thanks to you, asshole."

Emrick's head tilted slowly until he was looking directly at me. His smile was dark and did nothing to make him seem more approachable or friendly. If anything, it did the opposite. "The truth was going to come out eventually."

"Well, I'm glad you had so much fun exposing it so dramatically," I grumbled, folding my arms across my chest. "We're not here to talk about me. We have some questions for you."

Before I could say anything further, Nikki stepped forward, her hands on her waist and weight on one leg, tilting her hip. "I want all the information you have on Rueben Cole."

Emrick's eyebrows flickered upward in a moment that betrayed his piqued interest. "Was he the one who killed Murphy?"

"Yes," she said flatly.

Emrick chuckled. "Of course he was. Murphy was nothing but trouble for him from the start... that's a long-term feud going on there." The dark smile returned. "Unfortunately for Cole, he couldn't hold his own once I took over. I heard he jumped ship a few weeks back, heading to another city where he didn't have to work so hard to wrangle with the new kid in town… *me*."

"Where did he go?"

"No fucking idea, and I don't care as long as he stays out of my city."

I expected Nikki to argue about Emrick's claim of *my* city, but she said nothing, her toe tapping impatiently on the carpeted floor while she watched Emrick. "What else can you tell me?"

He leaned back in his chair, his large arms falling to the sides and impressive chest on display. His hoodie wasn't zipped up all the way, and he wasn't wearing a shirt underneath it. "Not much."

"Tell me what you *do* know," Nikki growled out.

Emrick stood, crossing the floor and closing the gap between them. To Nikki's credit, she didn't budge, although I made sure to move in behind her, ready to snatch her out of harm's way if Emrick tried anything. But he simply cast me an amused glance before returning his stare to Nikki. "You'd fetch a handsome price, you know," Emrick purred, lifting a lock of her blonde hair and letting it trail through his fingers. Nikki snarled at him and twisted to the side, pulling her hair from his hold.

Reaching around Nikki's shoulder, I snatched at Emrick's arm, and he cast me another disinterested glance. "I'd remove your hold of me, Cade, if you want to keep that arm." I did, but with a shove that jolted his shoulder back and forced a growl from his throat.

"Do you have any useful information or not?" Nikki demanded.

"Not," Emrick stated. "Only that he's been doing what he does for a long time, and he's good at it. If he doesn't want to be found, you won't be able to find him." He chuckled. "Hell, your own *father* ran half the crime in his fucking city, and you were so clueless you went and became a *cop*."

Nikki took a half step forward, shrugging her arm out of my grasp when I went to hold her back. She pressed a finger against Emrick's chest, and he tilted his head, gazing at her over his dark sunglasses, his black eyes blazing with rage and challenge.

"I'm going to find Cole..." Nikki whispered, holding his eye contact even though I could see her other hand trembling, "... and then I'm coming for *you*."

EPILOGUE

NIKKI

Eight Months Later...

Found him.

Flicking a switch on the dash, the police car siren let out a warning *whoop-whoop,* a fleeting but piercing sound that couldn't be ignored. My target was strolling along the sidewalk, hands shoved in his pockets and head ducked down, trying to make himself look small despite his rather considerable stature—all height and muscles. He paused midstep at the sound of the siren but didn't stop and continued making his way down the sidewalk. There were a few other pedestrians around who turned their heads to watch as I rolled the vehicle alongside the man.

"Sir, stop and raise your hands," I said, leaning

across the passenger seat and projecting my voice out the window. He said nothing and kept walking. Grabbing the mic from the dash, I repeated the command through the speakers, the crackling and volume grabbing the attention of the few remaining witnesses who had previously pretended not to notice.

His shoulders tensed, and slowly he withdrew his wisely empty hands from his pockets and unenthusiastically raised them above his head. Stopping the vehicle, I exited and came up behind him, one hand braced over my weapon in case he made a move. But he stayed still and didn't flinch when I grabbed his arms and cuffed his hands behind his back.

"Is this really necessary?" He drawled, a cross between amusement and boredom.

"You're hardly in a position to be asking me questions. Get in the car."

With a sigh, he allowed me to lead him to the rear door, and placing a hand on his head, I guided him to duck as he entered. His hands remained behind his back, and he slid into the seat until his arms found the wedges that allowed him to sit back, at least partially comfortably.

Pulling back into the traffic, he watched me through the rearview mirror, and every time I'd glance up, his dark eyes would be watching me, studying me. We drove in silence for a few minutes before he finally spoke up. "Where are we going?"

"Shut it."

He didn't seem put out by my attitude and simply raised a dark brow at me before looking out the window. I pulled the car into an underground parking garage, almost empty, and parked. Stepping out of the vehicle, I opened the door to the back seat and got in next to the man, making sure to leave the door unlatched. They didn't open from the inside.

"What are you doing?"

"Shh..." I muttered gently as I pulled my pants off, straddling him in only my underwear. "Cade," I whispered, smirking as I ran my fingers through his hair, "Poor, poor Cade. Cuffed in the back seat of a cop car, whatever are you going to do?"

He returned my grin. "If I weren't bothered about getting you in trouble, I'd snap these cuffs as easily as I did the last time you tried to restrain me like this."

I hummed. "I'm impressed you could keep control of yourself for as long as you did then." Tracing circles on his chest with my finger, I leaned forward and whispered in his ear, "Considering my lips were around your cock."

Cade's groan turned into a growl. "What is this, Nikki?" He fidgeted against the cuffs. "Get me out of these so I can fuck you."

Running my finger across his bottom lip, I

followed the gesture with my tongue, snapping my head back when he tried to steal a kiss before he followed it through with another growl. There was genuine aggression this time, and if I didn't have complete trust in the man between my legs, I'd have been concerned, but Cade had been nothing but protective. However, sometimes he was *too* protective, and it was time to remind him we were on equal footing in this relationship.

Besides, I doubted he'd hate the way I planned to teach him.

Cade and I had become a team, and while he still worked for Smithy moving furniture—although I told him my wage would support us both—he refused to not work. But when possible, he'd tag along for callouts, sticking to the shadows and almost disappearing in a way I found both thrilling and fascinating. Given how much of the crime in this city had demon involvement, Cade would be there if I needed him as backup, and if my partner asked, Cade was simply in the right place at the right time.

So far, it hadn't been an issue. But one day I might come across someone I couldn't handle, and Cade would be there. That would be the time I wouldn't mind his possessive and protective nature, although truth be told, it turned me on something fierce. I couldn't tell him that because it would give him all the power. But given the way his eyes flashed when I was aroused by his nature, I'm certain he already knew.

"You're going to stay cuffed…" I muttered, keeping my lips close to his neck and loving the way he shuddered with anticipation, "… and you're not going to break them, even when I'm riding your cock so fucking hard you come inside me."

"*Fuck,* Nikki…"

Shushing him gently again, I ran my tongue along his bottom lip, and this time when he stretched his neck forward to kiss me, I let him, opening my mouth and inviting his tongue in to play with mine. When his breathing became heavy, I reached up and wrapped my fingers around his throat, gripping. The rumble of his growl vibrated against my hand, and we moaned together as I traced my fingers down his body, hastily undoing his pants and releasing his cock.

"Commando." I chuckled. "Nice."

"I must've known my angel would be ready for a fuck today."

"You know I'm always ready for you."

Sliding my panties aside, I dipped a finger in my waiting pussy, moaning and gripping my hand harder around Cade's throat.

"Nikki, don't tease me, angel," he pleaded, his eyes trained on where my hand disappeared between my legs. I lifted my fingers to his mouth, and he breathed in deeply, groaning again as I slid my fingers over his tongue, making him taste my arousal.

Cade's eyes were heavy with lust as I positioned myself over him, teasing the head of his cock with my wetness before ever so slowly lowering myself onto him. When only the head was inside me, I watched his face, his jaw taut and eyes trained on mine, flashing with both irritation and pleasure.

"You're in so much trouble when you get home tonight," he growled out, bucking his hips up and penetrating me another few inches. I gasped, grabbing his shoulders to steady myself. "Unless you want to lose another set of handcuffs, I suggest you let me go."

"You really are no good at letting go of control, are you?"

Cade adjusted in the seat and thrust up into me again. I wasn't ready, crying out and grasping onto his jacket, the leather creaking under my grip. This was supposed to be my show, and somehow even handcuffed in the back of a police car, Cade was still taking control. I wanted him to. I wanted to let him out and bend over for him, submitting to his power and letting him fuck me through several orgasms. But I started this game, and I wasn't going to let him win that easy.

Although when he won, I did too.

Sliding down, I took him inside me fully, and we moaned in unison as my hips became flush with his. Leaning forward and wrapping my arms around his neck, I kissed along under his ear as I rode him, bouncing on his cock as he growled and shuddered again.

"Cade," I panted out.

"Yes, angel?"

"Tell me you love me."

Cade's voice was deep and soothing, his hard body against mine the perfect pleasure as he penetrated me. I'd never get enough. Each time I came with him, I only wanted more, and the time we had together before I went back to work was bliss—days and nights spent together naked in bed, fucking until we passed out then waking and going again. "You know I love you, Nikki."

I hummed next to his ear, increasing my rhythm and loving the sharp intake of breath as he hit a new angle inside me. He was getting close, so was I, and the rub of my clit against him with every thrust was ecstasy.

"I love you too, Cade."

His cheek moved against mine as his lips curled into a smirk. "Of course you do."

I chuckled, leaning back and changing moves until I was grinding against him in a slow rhythm. His eyes closed, and his head dropped back against the seat, but the smirk stayed in place. I had slowed down when he wanted it hard and fast, his arms tensed, and he fought the urge to break the handcuffs holding him back.

His smirk changed into a snarl as a growl escaped his throat. "Oh, you are in *so* much fucking trouble later."

I waited until he looked at me, a smirk on my face, then purposefully clenched my pussy walls around him, making him groan again. "I'm counting on it."

The **END**

Next in the Unearthly Sins Series
The Demon in Him

ACKNOWLEDGMENTS

Thank you, Jason, for comforting me with the words, "I'm sure it's not that bad." Making me do that watery chuckle / laugh-cry thing when he found me crying while writing this novel.
I don't like torturing my characters, you know.

Thank you, Kate and Ashleigh, for the specific medical-related queries I had for this book. I'm thankful to have people I can ask rather than flooding my internet history with some seriously dodgy searches.

And for everyone who fell in love with someone, and then years later you found out the terrible truth about them...
... that they are, in fact, *not* a supernatural being. Ripped off, right?

Connect WITH ME ONLINE

ANGELS AND FIRE BOOKS

Find our exciting stories at:

www.angelsandfirebooks.com.au

READER GROUP

Want access to fun, prizes and sneak peeks?
Join my Facebook Reader Group.
https://www.facebook.com/groups/588038442170571

NEWSLETTER

Sign up for my Newsletter.
https://www.subscribepage.com/angelsandfirebooks

BOOKBUB

https://www.bookbub.com/authors/stefanie-dawn

GOODREADS

Add my books to your TBR list
on my Goodreads profile.
https://www.goodreads.com/author/
show/21761217.Stefanie_Dawn

AMAZON

https://www.amazon.com/author/stefaniedawn

WEBSITE

http://www.angelsandfirebooks.com.au/

INSTAGRAM

https://www.instagram.com/angelsandfirebooks

EMAIL

info@angelsandfirebooks.com.au

FACEBOOK

https://www.facebook.com/stefaniedawnwriter

About THE AUTHOR

Stefanie Dawn has been a writer and creative soul all her life **and** strives to give her readers stories they can escape into as they become absorbed in the worlds created.

When she isn't writing, Stefanie might be painting, reading, or watching movies. She loves the process of producing films as another form of storytelling. There's also a good chance she'll be baking some delicious treats—pretending she won't later regret consuming them—or simply enjoying a cocktail with friends.

Stefanie Dawn lives in South Australia with her ever-supportive partner and a lovable gang of rescue cats.

You can stay up to date with
Stefanie and her books at:
www.angelsandfirebooks.com.au